# THE POPULARITY SUMMER

Joleen was clearly fascinated. "Frannie, I just can't believe all those exciting things happened to you because of a—plan."

Frannie propped herself on one elbow, suddenly not a bit sleepy, but excited by a new idea. Well, maybe not a *new* idea. . . . "Hey, we could try the plan with you!"

'*I can't do that!*" Jo wailed, throwing back the bedcovers.

Frannie reached out for Jo's trembling hand. "Listen, boys are human, after all. They're not as scary as you think, and they even have some of the same thoughts we do."

"I know the plan sounds crazy, but it works," Frannie added, grinning. "I'm living proof."

# The
# Popularity
# Summer

Rosemary Vernon

## BANTAM BOOKS
### TORONTO • NEW YORK • LONDON • SYDNEY

RL 6, IL age 11 and up

THE POPULARITY SUMMER
*A Bantam Book / August 1982*

ISBN 0-553-22682-7

*Published simultaneously in the United States and Canada*

*Bantam Books are published by Bantam Books, Inc. Its trademark,*
*consisting of the words ''Bantam Books'' and the portrayal of a rooster,*
*is Registered in U.S. Patent and Trademark Office and in other countries.*
*Marca Registrada. Bantam Books, Inc., 666 Fifth Avenue, New York,*
*New York 10103.*

PRINTED IN THE UNITED STATES OF AMERICA

0 9 8 7 6 5 4 3 2 1

# Chapter One

"What do you want to do tonight, Ronnie?" Frannie asked, pausing from their work as she watched her boyfriend thumbtacking a large poster onto a school bulletin board.

Ronnie shrugged but never missed a beat with his tacking. Frannie caught the muscle twitch in his left cheek as he replied, "I don't know, what do you want to do?"

She took a deep sigh, shaking her honey-blond head in a gesture of impatience as the voice within her screamed: *Same old question, same old answer, same old weekend scenario, starring Frannie Bronson and Ronnie Schell, same old couple that was supposed to be different. . . .* But she said simply, "We go through this every week, Ronnie—

exactly the same conversation. We ought to just tape it and play it every Friday."

Ronnie stopped, a thumbtack poised above the poster, which he had drawn. As he held on to one side of the poster, the other side began to dangle. He ignored it as he studied Frannie. "What are you talking about? Of course we go through this every weekend because we have to make our own plans whenever there's nothing special going on. What's wrong with that?"

Always the practical one, lamented Frannie silently. His dark brown hair dropped untidily over one smoke-gray eye. In the last year, Ronnie's face had filled out, losing what Frannie called its "hungry leanness." His physique had become very manly in the past few months, too, and Frannie had noticed how other girls were admiring him lately, though she pretended to ignore their attentions.

Well, what *was* wrong with asking the same question every Friday? Frannie wondered, a feeling of discontent stirring within her. "It's just that we usually end up going to a movie or to the Friday dance."

"At least we have a choice," Ronnie muttered. "Now will you please hold the other

2

end of this thing?" He nodded at the dangling end of the poster.

The poster, a drawing of a bright-haired couple dancing in the moonlight, announced the upcoming Graduation Party, which Frannie and Ronnie would be going to. Ronnie's artwork, well known around school, was sensational in Frannie's estimation.

She moved beside him, their shoulders brushing as they fitted the poster into place. His touch was so familiar to her now, she no longer spiraled off into never-never land every time their fingertips touched. She wondered if it was the same way for him. Of course, they shared so many interests, especially their artwork, which had drawn them together in the first place—if you didn't count the Popularity Plan.

If you asked Frannie's closest friends—Charlene McDaniels, Patti Davis, and Valerie Sanders—what had brought Frannie Bronson and Ronnie Schell together, they would answer, "The Popularity Plan, of course!" Because they were founders of the idea, they believed that every good thing that had happened to Frannie afterward was a result of their plan.

Before her friends had come up with the Plan, Frannie had been so shy she couldn't even ask a boy about a homework assignment. Her voice just jammed in her throat, and she stood there red-faced, unable to say a word. So for each schoolday, Charlene, Patti, and Valerie had come up with a plan that would start the shy Frannie talking to boys. They had thought of such ideas as dropping books at a locker so a boy would pick them up. Frannie had protested, but it had worked. There was the day Charlene had snitched Page Garvey's biology book and poor Frannie had had to return it to him herself, saying she had "found" it—one of the very worst scenes ever! But one good thing about the crazy plan was that it did start Frannie talking to boys. She actually overcame her terrible shyness and, as the plan originally promised, became very popular.

Frannie was still grateful to her friends for teaching her that one skill, since with Ronnie being nearly as shy as she was, they might never have gotten together at all.

Yet now, searching his face, she wondered where they had come to. They had been going together for fourteen months, their days falling into a predictable pattern—something Frannie had yearned for at first but now discovered herself fighting. Where had the romance, the spontaneity of their relationship gone? Was it still there somewhere, buried under the layers of familiarity? Frannie couldn't tell anymore.

*This is our relationship*, she reminded herself bitterly. *Me standing here, a tack between my teeth, holding up the other end of Ronnie's poster. Me thinking all these crazy thoughts while he is probably content with what he's doing right now.*

"What are you thinking about?" Frannie asked, knowing the answer before it came.

"I'm thinking that we ought to get all these posters hung in a hurry so we can get home, clean up, and eat dinner in time to go out tonight," he said, somewhat irritably.

"There're only two more to go," she reminded him. "No need to get impatient."

"Ouch!" Ronnie pulled his hand back abruptly as a petal of blood appeared on his index finger. "See what you made me do?" he grumbled, sucking on it.

"Let me see if you're hurt," she offered, welcoming the chance to take care of him. At least that was something different.

"How hurt can I get from a thumbtack, Frannie?" he cried, holding his hand out of her reach.

She shook her head in dismay. Silently, they finished hanging the rest of Ronnie's posters. She knew she got on his nerves sometimes, or got in his way, too; but she was powerless to know how to solve that little problem or understand how it had sprung up in the first place.

After they hung up the last poster, Ronnie drove Frannie home. As they pulled up in front of the house, Ronnie said, "I'll pick you up around seven, OK? How's a movie sound to you?"

Frannie had guessed he'd choose the movie since he didn't care much for dances. "Oh, sure, fine."

She would have liked him to kiss her goodbye, but her mother was at the mailbox, sifting through letters. As well as her parents knew Ronnie by now, Frannie still felt funny kissing him in front of them.

Joan Bronson looked up and waved to the couple in the car. "Hi, Frannie! Hi, Ronnie!" She started toward the car as the couple got out.

Ronnie shaded his eyes from the sun and smiled at her. "Hi, Mrs. Bronson. Any good mail?"

"Something for Frannie—from Aunt Joyce.

I wonder what it could be." She handed Frannie the letter, anticipation glowing in her perfectly oval face, framed by ginger-brown hair held back with two bright combs. She and Frannie had many of the same facial features—upturned nose, wide-set eyes, creamy complexion.

"You want me to open it now, right?" Frannie teased, rolling the corner of the envelope between thumb and forefinger.

"Open it," urged Ronnie.

"The suspense is killing me," admitted Mrs. Bronson, but she wasn't the only one. Rarely did Frannie receive a letter addressed just to her from her mother's younger sister.

Dear Frannie,

I hear you're doing really well in school and have a boyfriend. Jane and Joleen are fine, yet Joleen is as shy, if not more so, than I remember you being! Poor girl—with such a noisy family, too!

The reason I'm writing is to invite you up for a couple of months this summer. Your mother mentioned to me that your dad won't be taking a vacation this year, and next summer Uncle Mort and I will be vacationing in Europe, if all goes well. We had wanted to invite you to celebrate your graduation next June, but wondered if instead you'd like to come one year early? It would be a vacation for you, and we'd love to have you join us. I'm sure you remember how beautiful Cherry Lake is during the summer, and there's a lot to keep you busy.

Do think about it and let us know soon.

Love always,

Aunt Joyce

Frannie's heart was pounding while she reread the letter aloud. Her mother and Ronnie stared at each other in amazement.

"What do you think, Frannie?" Ronnie finally asked.

"I—I don't know. I mean, I only just got the letter!" Her hands were trembling.

"You've never been away from home before, dear, but I suppose there's always a first time." Mrs. Bronson's deep sigh made it clear to Frannie that her mother wished the letter hadn't come.

"I'd better be going. I'll see you later," Ronnie said gruffly, then got back into his car and gunned the motor.

Frannie waved goodbye absently and,

holding the letter close, walked inside with her mother.

"I'll be going to college in a year, anyway, Mom, so it'd help me to get used to being away."

"That's true."

She thought of Ronnie. Life without Ronnie for nearly a whole summer—could she stand it? Of course, she had lived without him for sixteen years before she met him—certainly she'd survive! And, she really did want a change in her life, didn't she? But maybe they would split up if they were separated for such a long time. Lots of couples did. Also, Ronnie was leaving for San Francisco State College in the fall, so if she went to Cherry Lake, they'd have hardly any time together this summer.

Still, Frannie bounced the tantalizing invitation back and forth like a Ping-Pong ball. Cherry Lake loomed in her memory as a jewel set in the rugged pine forest of the Sierras—smooth as glass in the early mornings, where not so much as a bird's wings ruffled its even surface. And along every shore was a strip of clean, white beach, different from Frannie's hometown beach where kids congregated in the summers. She remembered couples strolling through tree-lined corridors in the moonlight, hands entwined, stopping every so often to kiss. She imagined scenes she could sketch, boat rides, snow-capped mountains, horseback rides. . . .

It all sounded so romantic—but Ronnie wouldn't be there to enjoy it with her, she reminded herself quickly.

"I think it's a great opportunity," her father said when he heard of the invitation. "As much as I don't want to lose Fran for the summer, I guess I've got to be unselfish here."

A heavyset man with slate-blue eyes and short-cropped blond hair, Sam Bronson wore an expression that was heightened by the cleft in his chin that deepened when he smiled. Frannie could tell he was sad-happy about the prospect, but she knew her father was always open to new ideas. After all, ideas were his business. He ran a local advertising agency.

"You've already made some plans for the summer, haven't you, Fran?" her mother asked, her tone carrying the gentle reminder that you don't just drop everything and go away for the summer.

"Oh, yeah. I know, Mom." Both were thinking of the summer job at Sempel's, where

Mrs. Bronson worked as a buyer. Frannie had been looking forward to being a salesgirl and making her own money this summer. Because her mother worked at the store, Frannie had gotten the job, and for that, Frannie was grateful. Most kids her age could only get jobs at the fast-food places where they ended up always smelling like french fries. "I could get a job up at Cherry Lake," Frannie suggested meekly. "It might not be as good as working at Sempel's."

"Probably not," her mother agreed. "The number of teenagers applying for summer jobs up there must be enormous, considering they have even less openings in a place like that."

"Maybe I can babysit or mow lawns." Then, seeing her mother's expression sag, she added quickly, "Hey, nobody said I was going yet."

"True."

All the way through dinner Mrs. Bronson was quiet. Her husband, however, babbled on about the importance of Frannie meeting new people and seeing more than the cozy little California seaside town where they lived.

Frannie's thoughts shifted to the plans she and Ronnie had made for the summer:

trips to art museums in the Bay Area, an art exhibition in Montalvo, the sandcastle competition that Ronnie entered every year, days spent together on the beach. Could she miss all that—especially Ronnie's sandcastle sculpture?

Still, she dearly wanted to go to her aunt's. If only her parents would give their blessing. . . .

As her mother studied her with a look of sudden longing, Frannie giggled nervously. "Hey, Mom, I haven't left yet! This is only an invitation, remember?"

"Oh, I know," she responded, managing a smile. "I was just thinking how grown-up you're getting. But it's your decision, Frannie. Entirely up to you."

It was still a source of amazement to Frannie's parents that their only daughter was growing into a young woman. Though Frannie realized they were highly protective, she felt there was something nice about all their concern, even if it was kind of embarrassing sometimes.

Leaving them to ponder her maturity, Frannie went to her room, which she was almost finished painting a rich blue. With the ladder propped in one corner, her desk and bed in the middle of the floor, it was pretty messy, but she had a mental picture of how it was going to look when it was all done. She liked decorating. That was another thing—she had to finish the bedroom, but that could be done before school ended, she figured.

Quickly she changed into a cream jumper and yellow T-shirt, brushed her hair, and put on a little makeup. There was just enough time to twirl in front of the mirror for a final, satisfied inspection before Ronnie rang the doorbell.

# Chapter Two

"Want some?" Ronnie thrust the big tub of popcorn at Frannie just as the lights dimmed inside the theater.

Frannie took a few pieces, not yet hungry after her mother's stuffed cabbage. It was a suspense movie, one that Ronnie had been waiting for a long time to come to town.

The buttery scent of popcorn and Ronnie's cologne wove a pleasant cocoon around Frannie, and she felt somehow comforted by the familiar scene. She and Ronnie were real movie fans and enjoyed many of the same old films, especially mysteries.

Those were some of the really good things about their relationship, yet after awhile that same familiarity made Frannie restless. Maybe they shared too much in common, she thought. And they always sat in the same place, the lefthand section of the theater, he on the left, she on the right. This night could have been any Friday night they'd spent together for the last year. Standard procedure.

After the movie, they went out for hamburgers and Cokes. Ronnie ordered for both of them, already knowing what Frannie would want. Any other time it wouldn't have bothered her, but tonight it did. He was so *sure* of her—there were no surprises left.

"Maybe I don't want a hamburger without onions tonight. Did you ever think of that?" Frannie whispered across the ivory Formica table top so no one else would hear.

Ronnie stared in surprise. "Really? You always order that."

"You haven't bothered to ask me for the last six months," Frannie snapped, then immediately felt ashamed when she saw Ronnie's confused expression.

"I—I'm sorry," she quickly amended. "The hamburger is just fine. I don't know why I said that."

Ronnie's expression shifted to one of concern. "Hey, what's wrong, Fran? You're really acting strange tonight."

"Oh, I don't know. Maybe my aunt's letter has something to do with it." She spoke carefully, not sure what his reaction might be. "What do you think about it?"

"A summer's a long time to spend away from home, unless it's for school or something," Ronnie replied thoughtfully. "Anyway, she should've asked you before you made other plans."

"My plans aren't solid yet, Ronnie," Frannie said softly.

"Oh, yeah? You're full of surprises tonight, Frannie." He took a hefty bite of his burger. "You're not seriously considering the trip, are you?"

"Well, I . . ." she stumbled, unsure of how to answer. She wasn't sure of *anything* anymore! She felt light-headed, confused. "I'm thinking about it, Ronnie. I'd love to go. I mean, wouldn't you? It's such an opportunity."

Ronnie slid a wayward tomato back under the bun before nodding a halfhearted agreement. "Yeah, I guess it is. I just thought—well, you know, I'll be going to San Francisco in the fall. Things are going to be changing."

"I know. But I know what the summer will be like around here—like it's been every year since grammar school."

"Nothing's really the same," he argued. "You've got a good job, right? And what about the museums we were going to take in?"

What could she tell him? She had thought of all those things already.

"I guess if you do decide to go I can send you a photo of my sandcastle entry," he added.

"I'd rather be there, but a picture is worth a thousand words," Frannie replied, and he smiled and reached for her hand. For the rest of the evening, they talked about art.

Later, in front of Frannie's house, Ronnie held her in his arms for a long while, caressing her as if trying to memorize her, his kisses long and searching. Frannie melted into the circle of his arms, the heat of his touch racing through her as she thought: *Everything's okay again—we are still in love.*

Ronnie kissed her one lingering, last time before they parted. The doubts Frannie had struggled with earlier now seemed to dissolve with his kisses, and she wondered how she could ever have thought he was no longer romantic.

"What a fabulous idea!" cried Charlene, Frannie's best friend, when she heard about

17

the invitation. "You've got to go, Fran. It's the chance of a lifetime."

"Think of all the cute boys you'll meet up there," mischievous, red-haired Valerie chimed in.

"I don't know about the cute boys, Val." Frannie shook her head. "Ronnie and I—"

"Oh, you and Ronnie are inseparable, I know." Charlene waved away any protests with a flick of her flaming fingernails. "Haven't you ever heard that absence makes the heart grow fonder? Every relationship needs something to perk it up after awhile, and I know yours and Ronnie's does."

That hit Frannie right where it hurt. How did Charlene know—did it show? she wondered, panicking. But last night Ronnie had seemed so romantic. . . .

"Do your mom and dad like the idea?" asked Patti, a tall, pretty brunette. "I know mine would be ecstatic to lose me for an entire summer."

The girls laughed, and Frannie rolled her eyes. "You know my folks—they'd like to put me in a cradle if they could. But they're being really great about this. Dad's even encouraging me."

"Then do it! Take the opportunity, Frannie!

18

We would, wouldn't we?" Charlene searched the faces of the other two for agreement, and they both nodded enthusiastically.

"I really want to," Frannie said wistfully.

"Then do it, do it, do it!" the girls chorused.

Frannie giggled. Little Frances Bronson, going away for nearly a whole summer? Who, a little more than a year ago, was afraid of her own shadow. How she had changed!

Charlene was sitting cross-legged on the plastic tarp that covered the carpet of Frannie's room. "Now that that's settled, let's get down to the rest of our business. What are we all wearing to the Graduation Party?"

Trust Charlene to always conduct a conversation as if it were a meeting. If some kids considered her a little overbearing, Frannie thought she was wonderful for taking the responsibility and keeping things running smoothly. Without Charlene's perseverance, the Popularity Plan never would have been successful, Frannie knew.

Charlene, Patti, and Val got all caught up in a discussion of clothes as they thumbed through magazines. Strangely enough, Frannie was only mildly interested in what she'd wear to the Graduation Party—her thoughts were miles away, at the lake.

"What are you wearing, Fran?" Val asked. They knew that Frannie was a terrific seamstress and always came up with something fabulous.

"Oh, I don't know. I haven't thought about it yet."

"*You*? Not think about clothes? Come on, get on the ball, sweetie. You're not regressing, are you?"

Frannie skimmed through the magazine but didn't see anything she liked. "I think I've got an old Vogue pattern somewhere that I could turn into a summer formal," she told them.

By the time they were ready to leave, each girl had decided on all the details of fabric, style, and color for her outfit. Val was going to try sewing hers, and Frannie knew that meant she would be consulted every seam of the way. Charlene and Patti planned to buy their formals and decided to shop soon, before the stores sold out of the nicest ones.

Frannie's thoughts were still on the summer. She considered how she would tell Ronnie of her decision. It really hadn't been all that hard to make, even though she'd made it appear that way to her friends. *Maybe I made up my mind the very minute Aunt Joyce's letter arrived,* Frannie mused, surprising herself. Why, she had never been so impulsive before!

## Chapter Three

For the next three weeks until graduation night, Frannie dreamed of Cherry Lake. As she had expected, Ronnie showed no enthusiasm about the trip, though he tried to hide his feelings.

Yet sometimes Frannie wished he would come right out and say what was on his mind, though she knew he wouldn't. When he kept his feelings closed up inside like this, she didn't know where she stood with him.

On graduation night Frannie sat with Ronnie's parents in the outdoor amphitheater, a horseshoe of cement benches around a concrete stage. She watched proudly as Ronald Christopher Schell received his diploma.

Her eyes followed Ronnie onstage a second time as he received the Departmental Honors in Art award. He looked so handsome in the sweeping black robe that a lump formed in Frannie's throat.

Patti was also graduating this year, and Frannie knew she would feel lonely next year without Patti at Lincoln High. Amid all the past weeks' excitement, Frannie had given no thought until now to Patti's leaving. Of course, she would still be in town, but it wouldn't be quite the same.

The party that followed was a gala affair held at a local Holiday Inn banquet room. There were succulent prime ribs, delicately broiled fish, crisp, colorful salads, and sautéed vegetables—and mellow music to dance it off.

Ronnie, a reluctant dancer, went through the motions mainly to please Frannie, which took a lot of the fun out of it for her.

Because the party was such a special occasion, Frannie's parents had allowed her to stay out far past her curfew, figuring she could sleep during the drive to Cherry Lake the next day. Early the next morning, Ronnie appeared on her doorstep, still sleepy from their late night out. He shifted awkwardly from one foot to the other, wearing a funny grin as he said, "I guess this is goodbye."

Frannie invited him into the backyard to talk. "I'll be back in two months," she said, giggling nervously, trying to reassure him and herself at the same time.

"I guess I'll miss you, Fran. I'd thought—well—" He dropped his gray eyes, trying not to betray his emotions. "We had so many plans for the summer, but then I suppose plans are made to be changed."

"Sometimes," answered Frannie softly, feeling a little guilty for causing that change. The breeze riffled the maple leaves above their heads and teased Ronnie's hair. "I really want to do this, Ronnie. It's important to me." She looked at him pleadingly, wanting so much for him to understand how she felt.

"Yeah, I know. You'd never stand in my way of doing anything I wanted to do. Just don't forget about me, OK? And don't stop painting, either," he added quickly, plucking a big leaf off the tree.

She laughed. "I won't do either of those things. I'll send you some sketches, OK?" She tried to cheer herself by imagining the fresh scenes she could draw at the lake.

Ronnie nodded. "I'll save the museum trips until you get back. And I'll send you a photo of my sandcastle entry."

"Oh, great. That's one thing I'm sorry to miss," she said, then realized how dumb that sounded. "And you, too, Ronnie," she added quickly, but it sounded tacked on, as if she didn't mean it, even though she did.

Ronnie leaned against the rough tree trunk, pulled Frannie to him, and kissed her gently on the mouth, then tipped her chin and kissed her eyelids, her cheeks, her forehead. For a while they just held each other close.

With Ronnie so caring, his breath fluttering raggedly against her ear, Frannie felt a moment's regret at leaving. But it passed quickly, replaced by a sense of excitement as she thought of the summer that lay ahead for her. She was amazed at how easily she could say goodbye to him.

"Not too much farther now. We're at five thousand feet," Mr. Bronson reported.

With the whole backseat of the station wagon to herself, Frannie enjoyed looking through the windows at the towering pines rushing past in a blue-green blur. As they ascended the mountain, the road became twistier, the terrain rockier, and the trees more tightly packed together, forming a cool, dark canopy over the highway that was a blessed relief from the heat of the valley they had just passed through. The four-hour drive to her aunt and uncle's was almost over, and Frannie was glad.

In twenty minutes they were on Clemens Road, where nearly identical log cabins hunkered under pine boughs, followed by a cleared area, where a number of modern homes had been built. The Windhams lived in this section. The bottom half of their home was flagstone and the top redwood planks. Tendrils of pink and violet bougainvillea curled up trellises on either side of the rock pathway leading to the front door. An ornate white birdbath stood in the center of the tiny lawn, and Joyce Windham had placed three fake birds around it.

"Hey, Aunt Joyce still has the birds out there!" Frannie said, laughing.

"And I bet they're still frightening away the real birds!" Mrs. Bronson chimed in. It was a family joke that Aunt Joyce kept the intimidating, stone-eyed birds despite the fact that no bird in the neighborhood would set its beak in that birdbath.

Joyce Windham was the same petite, vivacious person Frannie remembered, except that now she wore her ginger hair in a curly perm. Her big gold hoop earrings and a huge brass pendant made her appear even smaller than she was. Her delicate features lit up when she saw Frannie, and she skipped over to the approaching station wagon like a young girl.

"Frannie, you look fabulous! Oh, my little niece is just precious, isn't she, Joan?" Mrs. Windham babbled on in her surprisingly loud voice.

Mort Windham's deep voice was equally loud. He was very rotund, and his eyes twinkled out of his pudding face as if he were always thinking up some new idea. Frannie had always heard what a wheeler-dealer he was. He was in real estate and never passed up the opportunity to try to sell a house.

"It's gorgeous up here, Mort. I love what you've done with the house," Mr. Bronson said.

"It's great country!" Mr. Windham boomed. "Like it? I can get you a house just about like this one for, say, eighty thousand, small down payment. Want to see it?" As Mr. Bronson protested, Mort Windham's laughter ricocheted off the trees. Between the two of them, Frannie imagined a person couldn't get a word in edgewise.

"Come meet the girls! It seems you have to reacquaint yourselves every time we get together—right, Frannie?" Joyce Windham led the way around to the back porch, where two slim girls were playing volleyball. The taller one fumbled the ball and had to retrieve it from the flowerbeds.

"Hey, Jo, what's with you?" her sister taunted.

"Jane, Jo, come see who's here!" Their mother's voice hit a high, warbling note, and Jane swiveled around.

"Frannie!" she cried, leaping with long strides across the lawn.

"Hi, Jane. Gee, you've grown!" Frannie cried, amazed at the transformation.

"I'm thirteen now," Jane said proudly.

Frannie grinned, remembering how good she herself had felt when she had become a teenager. Then she turned toward her other cousin. "Hi, Joleen."

Joleen was very tall and willowy with dark, straight hair pulled into a severe ponytail. Under straight, dark eyebrows was a pair of the loveliest green eyes Frannie had ever seen. "Hi," she replied, focusing on her bare feet.

This was the shy one, Frannie remembered, even though she'd never thought of

Joleen that way before—back when she was very shy herself.

"Joleen's sixteen now. Isn't she growing gorgeous?" Mrs. Windham prattled, unaware that Joleen cringed at every word about her. "I keep telling Mort that girl ought to get out and get involved. . . ."

Frannie's aunt chattered on obliviously, while Frannie observed her two very different cousins. Jane seemed a lot like her parents—bright, charming, bubbly—while Jo was just the opposite—withdrawn, pretty, and terribly shy. Frannie could tell she would have to make the first move with Joleen, which was the one thing that had always been so hard for her to do in all her relationships.

"I can see we're going to have to get to know each other all over again," Frannie began, noticing the red highlights amid the dark forest of Joleen's ponytail. "People change during two years."

"I'm in junior high now," piped Jane. "And I'm trying out for yell girl next year. Everybody says I've got a great chance," she added, giggling, "since I've got a great set of lungs."

"I imagine you do," Frannie said politely. Jane was definitely not shy. She turned her attention to Jo. "So you'll be a sophomore next year?"

"Junior," Jo corrected softly, her face turning beet red.

There was a moment of awkward silence, then Mrs. Windham said, "Hey, Jo, Jane, why don't you show your cousin around inside? I'm sure she'd like to see where she's going to sleep."

The girls led the way into the house, which was decorated in the loud oranges and yellows Joyce loved. She liked a house filled with sunshine, she said, but Frannie thought she'd gone a little overboard. Wall-to-wall orange carpeting covered every floor except the kitchen, which was done in spotted yellow linoleum. All the upholstered furniture was orange, with the only relief coming from the soft shade of the Early American dining room set and the other maple pieces in the living room. It amazed Frannie how much her aunt's style differed from her mother's subtle taste.

"This is Jane's room. Yellow, of course," said Jo with amusement, waving her hand toward the yellow, flower-sprigged curtains and the buttercup gingham spread.

Frannie's gaze met hers, and they both giggled.

"Hey, what're you two laughing at?" Jane asked, eyeing them with suspicion.

"Mom's and your fetish for yellow," Jo told her.

"Well, I didn't decorate this room," Jane announced. "Sure, I like yellow. But if I had my choice, I'd have it be"—she thought for a minute—"pink."

"You'll be sharing my room," Jo said shyly as she opened the door to a white room with blue calico curtains and matching bedspreads. Family photographs dotted the polished mahogany dresser, and an antique oval mirror hung above it. A stained-glass parrot dangled from a chain over the white desk with its matching rattan chair. It was a pleasant change from the rest of the house, and its simplicity immediately relaxed Frannie.

"This is where you'll sleep." Jo pointed to the bed next to the closet.

"Oooh, this is so cute!" Frannie walked around looking at everything. "I love this room."

Jo looked pleased, in a shy way. "It's not yellow, anyway."

They both laughed again, and while Jane

looked at them as if they were crazy, Frannie and Jo unpacked Frannie's suitcases.

Frannie had a feeling she was going to like her cousins, especially Joleen. Of course, she reasoned, it was easy to feel close to Jo—she had been so very much like her, not very long ago.

# Chapter Four

"I took the liberty of inquiring at Preston's, the art supply shop downtown, Frannie. Ted Preston said a boy just quit, so I told him what an artist you are. He'd like you to come by and talk to him." Mort Windham winked at Frannie across the dinner table.

She blushed at her mother's amused expression, which seemed to say, "OK, this is what you asked for—summer-long meddling." But there was no doubt about it, an art supply shop would be the perfect place for her to work, Frannie thought.

"I did want to get a job, Uncle Mort, and you know I'm familiar with a lot of supplies," she responded excitedly. "I'll check on it tomorrow."

Mr. Windham beamed. "Super! I'll drop you there on the way to the office in the morning, or Jo can drive you. Can't you, Jo?"

"Yes, Daddy." Jo hunched forward over her Caesar salad and barbecued chicken, as if she'd rather not be noticed.

"Joleen has a couple of friends you might like to meet, Frannie. Karen and Darla," Mrs. Windham said, smiling at Joleen.

"Creeps," muttered Jane.

"They're not creeps!" Jo shot back.

"Now, girls, don't fight in front of company," Mrs. Windham warned. "Karen would be a real sweetheart except every time a nice boy comes up to Joleen, Karen steps in and botches it."

"Mom, that's not true!" Flames crept into Joleen's cheeks as she defended her absent friend.

"Oh, come now, Jo. Maybe you don't see it, but your father and I do. And Darla—well, she's just not quite all grown-up yet, I'm afraid." Joyce uttered a meaningful sigh, the significance of which Frannie was not quite sure.

"She's fifteen years old and still wears a training bra," Jane said, sneering.

"My friends are pretty strange, too, come

to think of it," Frannie said, hoping to steer the conversation away from Jo's friends so the poor girl could relax. She launched into a description of Charlene, Val, and Patti, although she didn't mention the Popularity Plan—the adults just wouldn't understand.

After dinner and a session of home movies, everyone went to bed. Frannie's parents were spending the night and driving back in the morning.

As she slid under the downy quilt, Frannie felt almost at home in the comfortable little bedroom. Joleen, who had looked thoughtful all evening, asked, "Do you have a boyfriend?"

"Yes, Ronnie. Ronnie Schell."

"What's he like?"

How to describe Ronnie to another girl? Frannie reflected. Her own friends had not been terribly impressed with him at first but had come to appreciate him after Frannie started dating him. "He's cute but shy, like me. He's a really great artist, too," she replied proudly.

"How long have you been going with him?" Joleen asked shyly.

"Well, I first went out with him around Christmas a year and a half ago. We've officially been going steady for fourteen months."

"How did you meet him?"

"Well, we were in the same art class, although he's a year ahead of me," Frannie said. "He just graduated. But I probably never would have even spoken to him if my friends hadn't made up this Popularity Plan to get me to talk to boys."

"Really? They actually thought up a plan? How'd they do it?" Jo was wide-eyed at the idea.

"I was really super-shy. I couldn't even say hi to a guy, so my friends decided it was time I got over it. They plotted little scenes . . ." She described some of the points of interest in the plan—the staged conversations, the dates, and the Halloween dance, where she'd won a prize for the most beautiful costume.

Joleen was clearly fascinated. "I can't believe it—I mean, it's too good to be true, isn't it?" She shook her head in astonishment. "You're really pretty, Frannie, and you're nice, but I just can't believe all those exciting things happened to you because of a—plan."

"They did, and they would've kept happening if I hadn't put a stop to it."

"Why would you want to do a thing like that?"

Frannie giggled. It did sound dumb unless

you knew the whole story. "Because Ronnie was shyer than I was after the plan started working, and I was dating all these different boys. I suddenly realized the attention I was getting might scare him off. Of course, I didn't even know if he liked me or not, but I liked him so much, I figured he was worth a chance."

"My friends wouldn't do anything like that for me. I mean, they're not the least bit popular. How'd you get popular friends when you weren't popular?"

"I made friends with Charlene one day...." Rather than tell her cousin how she had seen Charlene crying by her locker one day over her parents' divorce, Frannie just described how they'd got to talking in the hall one day after school in junior high and how from then on they had become friends.

"We never planned it," Frannie went on. "It just happened." She grew quiet, contemplating her cousin's wistful gaze. "Is there anyone special for you?"

"No—well, yes, but he doesn't know I exist. I can't talk to boys, either." Jo blushed. "He's really popular, and—well, I like him, but I'd never stand a chance with him."

"Every girl stands a chance," Frannie

replied. "Especially someone like you, Jo. You're cute, smart, and nice." *Haven't I heard that somewhere before*? she thought, recalling Charlene's very words to her.

Joleen began to protest, but Frannie propped herself on one elbow, suddenly not a bit sleepy. She was excited by a new idea. Well, maybe not a *new* idea. . . . "Hey, we could try the Popularity Plan with you! Although I don't know if I'm the one to do it. I wish Charlene were here."

"You couldn't do that with *me*! Oh, no! Peter is dating a girl already—she's beautiful, Frannie. Wait until you see her. Sandi Sloan."

Frannie sighed. How much of an obstacle was this girl? If they were steadies, it would be really hard to get Peter interested in Joleen, but then Jo might be making more of the relationship than there really was.

"Beauty isn't everything, although it does count for something," Frannie counseled. "But you're beautiful, too, in your way. You have gorgeous hair, and your eyes are fantastic. We could make you look absolutely stunning and teach you how to talk to boys."

"I can't do that!" Jo wailed, throwing back the bedcovers.

"Listen, if I can do it, *anybody* can."

Frannie wagged a finger at Jo, who appeared only half convinced. She reached out for Jo's trembling hand. "Please believe me. Boys are human, after all. They're not as scary as you think, and they even have some of the same thoughts we do." She paused, concentrating. "Now we'll have to decide on our approach. You let me know what kinds of activities go on around here, and then we'll set up scenes where you have to say something to a guy. It doesn't have to be much, just 'hello,' 'excuse me'—anything. You'd be surprised how little it takes to start a conversation."

Joleen frowned.

"I know it sounds stupid, but it works," Frannie added, grinning. "I'm living proof."

# Chapter Five

The next morning Frannie felt depressed as she watched her parents drive off, though she tried to hide it around Joleen and the vivacious Jane. Her mom had warned her to take her vitamins, eat properly, go to bed at a "decent" hour, and not to catch a chill. Then the familiar brown station wagon carried her parents out of sight, leaving Frannie with the sudden strange realization she wouldn't be seeing them for a whole summer. She bit her lip against a crop of tears.

Sensing Frannie's distress, Joleen remarked, "I've never been away from home before, either. When I was eleven I turned down a trip to summer camp, and my folks and Jane thought I was crazy. Jane went, of course."

"Sounds like something I'd do," Frannie said. "Still, it doesn't help when you're a senior in high school and still miss your mommy and daddy."

They burst into giggles.

Then Joleen drove Frannie into town to Preston's, where Frannie talked to the owner. They went on to the local department store next, where they decided on a swimsuit for Joleen. Once in the store, Frannie felt better and began outlining her ideas for the plan while Joleen plucked suits off the rack to take into the dressing room.

"The first stage is to get you a cute suit and a neat towel and beach bag. Your mom said you're not big on clothes."

"I can't see what all the fuss is about," Jo replied.

Frannie pulled a small memo pad out of her nylon zippered bag. "You'll see. Now you're going to have to tell me some things about Peter, since we're mostly concerned about getting him interested in you. My friends got several boys interested in me, and we can use that tactic, too. Peter will notice you if everyone else does."

Joleen's smile was more of a grimace. "Peter's tall, with dark, curly hair and eyes.

He's smart, too, and last year he was the junior class president and on the debate team. I don't know if he's got a summer job, although his dad runs a boat supply store."

"Maybe Peter works there," suggested Frannie, busily jotting down the facts.

"Maybe. But he spends nearly every afternoon at the beach or out in his boat. There's a place called the Canteen where they hold dances on Friday nights, and some nights they have movies. I know he's taken Sandi to the dance a couple of times."

"Is that all? You made it sound like they were going steady." Frannie shook her head but was secretly relieved that the competition was not as stiff as she had suspected. "What's Sandi's personality like?"

"I don't really know her, but Darla calls her a snob."

Frannie wrote "possible snob" next to S.S. She used initials in case the notebook got lost. She didn't want to risk hurting somebody's feelings because of a rumor. "Maybe we'd better make our own deduction on that one. What other activities are big around here?"

Frannie's past stays at Cherry Lake had been limited to one or two days, so she wasn't familiar with everyday life at the resort town.

"Water skiing, picnicking, swimming. The popular kids all meet at the beach and then go on from there. Everybody who is anybody knows the day's plans."

"So we'll make it our business to find out, too. Not that we'll follow them, but we'll follow Peter's day pretty closely. That's what we'll do today, OK? We have to know where he'll be at all times. Then we can build the plan around him." Frannie glanced up from her notes to behold her cousin in a silky green bikini. "That looks sensational on you, Jo! I'm sure you'll attract more boys than you can stand."

"Oh, yeah—they'll be beating down my door," she muttered. "Do you really think this looks good?" Joleen surveyed herself with a critical eye. Frannie knew how she felt—it was hard to believe you could look good, so you needed someone else's opinion to sort of ground you to the reality.

"Honest—the guys will be overwhelmed!"

Frannie helped Joleen choose a beach cover-up, a dark green shift, and then they bought a lush velour towel with big green cats printed on it.

"I'll look like the Jolly Green Giant," Jo grumbled.

"No you won't," Frannie insisted. "You're going to be stunning. The crazy towel will establish you as a person with a great sense of humor."

"Oh, sure. I'm a barrel of laughs."

"You're going to surprise yourself, Joleen Windham," Frannie promised, laughing. The Plan was becoming more exciting for her than it was for Joleen. Now she understood why Charlene had enjoyed it so much.

When they finished shopping, Frannie asked Joleen to drive past Peter's father's store. Reluctantly Jo agreed, parking way down the street while Frannie peered in the store window like a casual tourist.

Above a window display of fishnets, cork, rusted lanterns, and ship parts, she glimpsed a tall, curly-headed boy with olive eyes who fit Jo's glowing description. He was standing behind the counter helping a customer with life preservers.

After jotting down this information, the girls went home to change for the beach and eat lunch. Jo's mother had left a plate of delicious cold chicken with the instructions *Eat for lunch* taped to the tinfoil covering.

There was a note on the refrigerator from Jane telling her mother she'd be at the beach all afternoon with Lisa, Bridget, and Vicki.

Jo showed Frannie her extensive stamp collection, explaining that the stamps had sparked her interest in geography and that now she was thinking that she might like to become a mapmaker, or cartographer.

"You'll be the only one I've ever known!" exclaimed Frannie, impressed by her cousin's ambition.

She helped Jo try some of her makeup, experimenting with a dark brown pencil that was too dark for her own eyes but was perfect for Jo's.

"You want people to notice your eyes," explained Frannie. "Remember, eyes are sort of like windows, so you should make them stand out. And now your hair. You've got a small face, and all that hair detracts from it a little. What do you think about cutting some off?"

Joleen cringed and thoughtfully studied a lock of her shining mane. "Well, I don't know. I've had it for so long . . ."

"Then maybe it's time for a change. You don't have to," Frannie assured her, not wanting to be pushy. After all, she wasn't like

Charlene, who would have whipped poor Jo down to the hair stylist's without a moment's hesitation. "It's just a suggestion. With only two inches off the length, your face could look fuller."

Jo shook her head in amazement. "How do you know all this stuff?"

"Let's just say my friends gave me an extensive education."

Jo laughed nervously. "OK, I guess two inches isn't much." Before she had time to change her mind, she made an appointment at the Clip Joint for the next morning.

Finally, the two girls strolled down to the beach, which stretched around the lake as far as the eye could see. On one side was a boat ramp, where several sun-bronzed teens pulled a speedboat onto a boat trailer. Some little kids were fishing off a pier nearby. And in the long shadows of the pines, several older people sat in folding patio chairs, while the teenagers gathered in one spot—around the lifeguard's tower. Without having to be told, Frannie knew that was the official meeting place.

"That's Jim Wiseman in the lifeguard tower," whispered Jo. "He's a big hero around here since he saved a couple of people from drowning last year."

"Really?" Frannie squinted at the slim blond figure lounging in the tower, studying him with interest. "I don't think I've ever met a hero before."

They walked nearer to the group, whose laughter and loud radios spread a carpet of gaiety all around them. Joleen looked increasingly uncomfortable, and, not looking where she was going, she tripped over a stone. Her beach bag went flying, spewing out towel, tanning lotion, hairbrush, and wallet. Frannie rushed over to pick them up, then handed the bag back to her cousin. "Are you all right?" she asked Jo.

Jo nodded without confidence. "I don't want to go over there."

Frannie glanced over at the group of happy kids.

*They might as well be posing for a Pepsi ad*, she thought. "Look. This is the perfect time for you to be showing me around. I'm new here, remember? Maybe you can introduce me to someone."

"I don't know these people, Frannie. They don't even say hi to me."

"Well, let's just pass them, smiling. Since

they don't know me at all, it's a perfect time to grab their attention," Frannie suggested. "They'll want to check out the new person on their beach, won't they?"

"Who wants attention?" Joe was really getting panicky. Frannie practically had to drag her along the beach.

*You'd think we were walking in the path of a speeding train,* Frannie mused as they neared the popular group. She kept talking, asking questions of Joleen, trying to keep her occupied with acting as tour guide rather than worrying about what the group would think or do.

There was nothing to worry about, anyway, Frannie was convinced. Out of the corner of her eye she glimpsed one of the girls passing out sandwiches to the others—they were all very preoccupied with their own affairs. The girl was a pretty, petite blond with a super tan. That was another thing Joleen needed—a tan.

Two girls with long, sandy hair brought Cokes from the snack bar and knelt down beside the blond. As Frannie and Jo walked past, Frannie heard one called Terry and another Sandi. She wondered if the blond was the Sandi that Peter had dated.

Frannie and Joleen slid past the group unnoticed and went over to a rocky part of the shore, where several boats were anchored. "This is where my dad keeps his boat," Joleen explained, pointing out the white hull with a glossy wooden interior. "See the white one with *Bunny May* on it? My mother keeps teasing him about Bunny May being an old girlfriend of his."

"Was she?"

"He says no, that Bunny May was his pet goldfish." Joleen pushed her toes into the warm sand. "The blond girl back there is Sandi Sloan, the one I told you about."

Frannie chanced a look down the beach, picking out a tall, dark-haired figure sauntering toward the group. If it hadn't been for the self-assured way he walked or his "body language," as Charlene referred to it, Frannie might have thought he was Ronnie.

"Peter!" Joleen whispered.

Frannie turned to find her cousin wide-eyed, her hand clutching her throat.

"Take it easy," Frannie urged. "Let's just walk slowly up the beach, past the tower again, very casually. Have you ever talked to Peter?"

"Once, in Spanish class. I asked him a question about conjugating verbs. It nearly killed me," admitted Joleen, "but the teacher was out of the room, and he was the only one not clowning around that I could get a straight answer out of."

"Sounds like a fascinating conversation," Frannie teased gently, for she knew what that was like. How many times had she swallowed questions for fear of voicing them in class? Or gotten up the nerve to ask a boy and then been so nervous about it she couldn't understand his reply?

The group loomed closer, and Frannie wanted to keep Jo from getting really uptight. "Do you still have the canoe you had last time I was here?" She raised her voice slightly.

"Y-yes, we still use it, too. I'll take you out in it someday, but I don't paddle very well," Jo said.

Frannie could hear her breath coming in quick, uneven gasps, and sneaking a sideways glance, she saw Jo's shoulders all hunched up.

"Relax!" Frannie ordered, reaching out and squeezing her cousin's wrist.

Wanting to arrive right in front of Peter when he was sure to notice them, Frannie gauged her steps, keeping a furtive eye on him as he laid down his towel, then flopped onto it, unmistakable in bright-red satiny trunks.

When they reached the edge of his towel, Frannie moved closer to Jo and knocked something out of Jo's beach bag.

For a split second Jo stiffened, her face turning the color of wallpaper paste. *Oh, no,* Frannie thought, *she's going to go back for it!* She elbowed Joleen, just hoping and praying the gesture wouldn't confuse her. Maybe it wasn't fair to spring this little trick on her but . . .

"Excuse me."

There was a tap on Joleen's shoulder. She whirled around and gasped, the color rushing back to her face. Peter Culp was smiling down at her, and in his outstretched palm lay her suntan lotion. Her expression switched from shock to a prize-winning smile, and Frannie sighed from her toes.

"I think you dropped this," Peter said, his voice deep and resonant, with none of the rough edges that many boys' have. He placed the plastic bottle in Joleen's hand and closed her fingers around it.

"I—I think so," she stammered, blushing prettily. "Thank you very much."

"You're welcome," he said, grinning.

Frannie watched her cousin melt before her eyes. Although Jo was still stiff and nervous, she looked pretty and natural facing Peter.

At that very moment, Sandi Sloan perked up and saw the same picture, and her face hardened into an angry scowl.

"See you around," Peter said, saluting Jo gaily.

"See you," parroted Joleen, falling numbly into step beside Frannie—except that Jo was floating two feet above the sand.

# Chapter Six

"I can't believe it!" Joleen kept repeating, eyes shining, as she floated along on her cloud.

"I told you so. See, he really noticed you," Frannie pointed out triumphantly, thinking how a few minutes earlier she had feared total disaster.

Joleen turned to her. "But without you, where would I be? I mean, I can't drop my own suntan lotion, can I?"

"Who says you can't? Anyway, we'll think up other ideas for you. You can't rely on dropping things. It looks too silly."

The wheels of Frannie's mind were already whirring away. She'd observed a cute girl walk up to the lifeguard tower and request a Band-Aid for her stubbed toe. Now, that was something Joleen could do easily enough, and it didn't even need much conversation. As they strolled along the pier, Frannie glanced into the bait shop and saw a young man winding fishline. There were boys working in the snack bar, too: good practice in conversation she figured.

They sat down at the water's edge, and Frannie took out her note pad.

"What're you doing?"

"Drawing up a schedule for you," explained Frannie. "Is there anyone you know who shares your interest in stamp collecting?"

"Only Darla."

"I mean boys."

"Not that I know of. It's not exactly the kind of hobby you run around bragging about. What's with 'Monday, Tuesday, Wednesday'?"

"Your schedule. Do you know how to fish?"

"Not really. This sounds more like a questionnaire," complained Joleen.

"Ronnie taught me how, so I'll teach you." Frannie grimaced as she remembered slicing off the heads of pile worms and lacing the squirmy bodies onto the hook. Ronnie had patiently taught her everything he knew, and together they'd gone out early in the morning to fish, before the sun was even up.

"I want you to go into the bait shop tomorrow and ask for some bait to use around here," Frannie instructed. "The boy in there will help you. Wednesday we'll go fishing. Thursday we'll go out in the canoe. Friday you'll ask the lifeguard for a Band-Aid. Saturday you will order a hamburger from that snack bar but make sure a boy waits on you."

"That sounds terrible!" Joleen cried. "I can't do any of those things."

"Of course you can. Remember today?" Frannie made a silly face, and Joleen's expression softened into a starry-eyed grin.

"Can we use your dad's boat Sunday?"

"I'll have to ask."

"If we can, we'll pretend we can't start the motor, and then you'll ask a boy to help. That may not work, but we'll give it a try, anyway." Frannie scanned her notes. "Oh, I forgot to mention, we're going to the dance Friday night."

"No! I can't dance!" Joleen wailed.

Frannie shook her head. "You'll learn fast."

"Well, if it isn't Joleen," came a sarcastic, whiny voice.

Joleen turned around with dread in her eyes. "Hi, Darla, hi, Karen," she greeted lifelessly, then introduced her friends to Frannie.

Darla, the whiny-voiced, mousy-haired one, had a thin, rigid face and cool gray eyes that seemed to stare right through Frannie. Although Frannie didn't like to rely on first impressions, she had a feeling that Darla liked to take advantage of people's faults. Jo was just the type of person too shy to resist Darla's pushy ways. Maybe Aunt Joyce had been right about her, Frannie reflected.

On the other hand, Karen seemed naively sweet, but all she talked about was horses, which, Frannie found out later, was all she was really interested in.

After babbling about the fabulous vacation she and her family were taking the following week, Darla sniped, "Well, it's about time you introduced us to your cousin. I was wondering when you were going to, Joleen."

Joleen turned crimson, while Darla whirled about, grabbing Karen, who waved a reluctant but still-friendly goodbye.

"Some friend," Joleen muttered when Darla was out of earshot. "I'm glad she's going away for the summer."

"Karen seems nice," offered Frannie, realizing she had nothing nice to say about Darla at all. "Back to business, here. We have to work on your tan. You look sort of like—" She fished around for a description that wasn't too uncomplimentary. Living by a beach, she had a golden tan already, but Joleen was positively white.

"The underside of a fish," supplied Joleen.

"We'll get some of that quick-tanning stuff for you," Frannie decided.

"Jane has a sunlamp, too."

When they returned to the house, Jo got the sunlamp. There was a phone call for Frannie from Preston's, asking her to come to work the following morning.

"Congratulations—but what about the plan?" cried Joleen.

"Listen, Jo, it's not that hard to ask the guy for bait. That's all you have to do. It wouldn't help having me there." Frannie tried to console her. "I'll be off at noon, and then we can go to the beach, OK?"

"OK," replied Jo sullenly.

They drove to the drugstore to pick up the lotion, then hurried home to catch the last rays of sun on the patio.

"What is that stuff?" demanded Jane, appearing at the screen door. "What did you do to your legs?"

Frannie and Jo looked up, startled. They followed Jane's gaze to their legs and torso, which were streaked orange.

"Oh, no! I hope this comes off!" Frannie began frantically wiping her legs with the corner of a beach towel. To her horror, it didn't.

"I wish I'd known you were going to use that stuff." Jane sighed knowingly. "It streaks, and you can't get it off for a while."

"For how long?" Jo scraped her skin with a fingernail in the hopes of removing the orange.

"A couple of days." Jane shrugged. "It looks worse on you than on Frannie. At least she's got a tan already."

Until that moment, Frannie had thought nothing could dampen her cousin's bright spirits, but now Jo angrily brushed past Jane and stomped into the house.

"You shouldn't have said that," remonstrated Frannie. "Jo didn't need to hear it."

Jane eyed her with confusion. "Why should it bother her? She's never cared that much about how she looks. Although now that you're here, maybe she will."

"Maybe she never had a reason to care before," Frannie snapped, remembering her own transition from sewing doll clothes and stuffed animals to taking an avid interest in her own wardrobe.

But the shrewd glint in Jane's eye warned Frannie that she'd better keep quiet. Although she was an only child, Frannie had learned from her friends' experiences that one could never trust a kid brother or sister with secrets— especially the romantic kind!

Hoping to console Jo, Frannie slipped into her bedroom. "It doesn't look that bad, Jo, really. And it'll go away," she said.

When Joleen didn't reply, Frannie got her diary and went out in the backyard.

Dear Diary,
    Here I am at Cherry Lake, helping my cousin with the P. Plan, when what happens but we get quick tan for her, and she turns orange! Ronnie will laugh when I tell him, not to mention Charlene.

Jane called out to her to come and answer the phone.

His voice startled her, and until that moment she honestly hadn't missed him very much. "Hi, Ronnie. What're you doing?"

"Thinking about you on that beach with all those strange guys. I haven't forgotten the 'plan,' you know." He was teasing her, but there was uncertainty in his voice.

"Ha-ha. Don't worry. My cousin needs the Plan now. We're doing one for her, and it's working!"

Ronnie was silent for a moment. "Oh, sounds great, Fran. But I thought it didn't work out all that well for you, I mean—"

"It did, and it didn't, Ronnie. But I've sort of revised it for Joleen, so we'll just have to wait and see. Remember, the Plan got us talking to each other, didn't it?"

"Yeah, well, I just don't want you talking to too many guys, I guess." He sounded unhappy.

"I haven't talked to anyone. Joleen's doing all the talking." She described Joleen, Peter, the orange legs, her aunt and uncle, Jane and the house, and then her job at Preston's.

"Sounds good. That's better than working at the T-shirt factory all summer," he said enviously, referring to the T-shirt booth he worked in at a local amusement park.

"I'm not sure yet," Frannie told him, not wanting the job to sound too wonderful. "I'll let you know how it turns out."

While Ronnie talked, a picture of Joleen and Peter came to Frannie's mind—slim figures silhouetted against dappled, dancing water—and an ache formed in her chest. Ronnie's days since she'd left had been so ordinary—his summer job, swimming, the old beach crowd that they always joked about, the mystery movie he was planning to see with his brother Paul tonight. If she were at home, Frannie would go to the movie with Paul and Ronnie. Paul would wisecrack throughout the film. Ronnie might drape his arm around her shoulders, but if Paul made fun of him, he'd remove his arm. Frannie realized she wasn't sorry to be here instead of at home.

"I'd better get off the phone," Ronnie said then. "This is costing me money."

"OK. Have fun tonight," she told him.

"Yeah. Chances are minimal with Paul. You take care of yourself, Fran," he mumbled softly, then hung up.

Franie stared at her orange-streaked legs and sighed. Funny, she felt like she'd disappointed Ronnie somehow; but also, she was slightly disappointed in the conversation herself.

What had she expected, anyway?

# Chapter Seven

Frannie's employer, Mr. Preston, was a jovial man with wiry, gray hair and beard, and a patch over one eye like a pirate. He told her he had injured his eye in a boating accident, but after one morning of learning the ropes of art supply along with listening to Mr. Preston's tall tales, Frannie wasn't so sure about the truth of his story.

Her job was to assist customers and, when things were slow, to straighten merchandise. She loved the smell of new pencils and charcoal, the crisp feel of watercolor paper, and the wood aroma of the easels. Mr. Preston said she'd get a twenty-percent discount on anything she bought there, so Frannie made a mental list of her art needs and couldn't wait until payday so she could buy something.

At noon her aunt picked up Frannie and dropped her at home on the way to meeting a friend for lunch. Frannie found Joleen in the bathtub, and there was an awful, fishy smell.

"What are you doing?" she asked.

"What does it look like? I'm taking a bath—getting the horrible smell of salmon eggs off my skin!" Joleen cried in disgust. "I went down to the bait shop after I got my hair cut. I asked for some bait, and this guy sold me the salmon eggs. He opened the jar to show me, and when he handed it to me, I dropped it. It spilled all over me—I felt like such an idiot!"

Frannie giggled. "Did he laugh?"

"Yes, and I ran away—I was so embarrassed!"

"He won't forget you easily, that's for sure!" Frannie replied, but that wasn't the kind of assurance Jo needed right then. "How'd the haircut go? Do you like it?"

"It's great." Joleen unpinned the freshly cut mass of thick hair from its crown so that it tumbled around her face in a smooth, shiny cascade.

"Much better," agreed Frannie, relieved that at least one thing had gone right this morning. "By the way, what was the boy's name?"

"Chip Daniels. He's in my geometry class."

"I guess we'll have to buy more salmon eggs."

"No, we won't. Chip gave me another jar, free," Jo gave her a sheepish look. "He told me not to worry, he'd clean up the mess, too."

"That was nice of him. He probably smells a little fishy himself by now." That dissolved Joleen's anger at herself and sent them both into giggles.

Joleen didn't want to be seen at the beach with her skin streaked orange, so she and Frannie sunbathed in the backyard, and Frannie gave her a dancing lesson.

The next morning, Joleen refused to go fishing without Frannie. "I don't want to be out there all by myself," she wailed. "I don't know what I'm doing, and I don't want to make a fool of myself."

Reluctantly, Frannie gave in. She really wasn't very good at giving people orders. "All right. I'll meet you back here after work, then. But it's important for you to be seen around. Tonight we'll go to the movie at the Canteen, OK?"

"OK."

After work, Joleen was ready and waiting, with a picnic lunch and the fishing poles, which her father had set up for her. They were trout poles, reedlike in comparison with the long, hefty ones Frannie and Ronnie had used for ocean fishing.

When they had settled themselves on the end of the pier, Frannie showed Jo how to put the salmon eggs on the hook so that the hook was concealed from the fish.

"This is yucky," Jo complained. "What do I do if I catch one?"

"Just reel him in," ordered Frannie, casting her line. Of course, she didn't want to let Jo know her chances of catching a fish were slim—lunchtime was a bad time to catch fish, as they generally ate in the mornings and evenings. Still, it gave Jo something to do fully clothed—the orange streaks still hadn't vanished—while checking out the beach scene at the same time.

"I overheard Jane mention that the gang was going boating today, maybe over to the other side of the lake," Frannie said. "Next time, if we're on the beach we might be able to get you invited to go along."

"Yeah, sure. They'd never invite me." Jo shook her head.

"Don't be so sure about that." Frannie noticed that some teenagers were on the boat ramp. One boy was backing a boat into the water, another shouting instructions. Frannie recognized the girl in a pink flowered bikini as Sandi Sloan. The boy getting out of the car was Peter Culp. He wore cutoffs and no shirt, so you could see his muscles rippling beneath his bronze skin.

Frannie nudged her cousin. "Guess who?"

Joleen followed Frannie's gaze, her eyes lighting up, then narrowing at the sight of Sandi toting the picnic basket. "Guess who's supplying the picnic lunch?"

Frannie patted her hand. "There's a Little Red Riding Hood in every crowd," she consoled. "At least ten in every crowd."

Just then Jo got a bite. "Reel it in, come *on!*" urged Frannie, her excitement mounting as the reel clicked away. Joleen trembled as her pole bobbed up and down. Finally a wriggling trout surfaced from the water.

The boatload of kids was just passing, and they broke into a cheer when they saw Jo's catch. The fish flopped around all over the wooden platform as Jo tried desperately to grab its slippery body. Suddenly she slid on the wet planks, lost her balance, and plopped into the water.

An explosion of laughter rocked the boat. Frannie lifted the line with the fish still hooked to it and wrapped it in her beach towel. A bedraggled Jo surfaced, and Frannie helped her onto the platform.

"You caught quite a fish, Jo!" she exclaimed, unwrapping the towel. "Look at him—about ten inches for sure. Your dad will be proud of you!"

"Oh, geez!" Joleen groaned, hiding her head in her arms. "What a scene I made."

"You mean what a splash. Everyone saw you—and the fish. It's great. Don't feel bad." It was easy for her to say, Frannie realized as soon as she'd said it, for if she'd done the same, she'd be embarrassed. Still, everyone had noticed Jo, and as the boat cut away with Peter at the tiller, Frannie couldn't help but notice his wide grin as he looked back at the drenched girl on the pier. When Joleen finally looked up, she saw him—seaman's cap cocked at a jaunty angle, his hand raised in a wave.

"Wave back!" Frannie ordered. "Let him know you see him!"

Jo's fingers lifted in a limp flutter of farewell, as if she were seeing her love ride off on the lake for the last time.

"You look like the heroine in some romance novel," Frannie said teasingly.

"Oh, cool it. I just waved. Didn't he look *good*, Frannie?" She was grinning.

"So did you. I just know you'd make a terrific couple."

That evening Joleen and Frannie went to a movie. Chip Daniels from the bait shop strode over just to say hi to Joleen, which, Frannie insisted, was a real plus.

On Thursday the two girls took the canoe out. Chip Daniels helped set it in the water, although it was certainly light enough for Frannie and Joleen to handle alone. Frannie quickly discovered that Joleen was very good at paddling. It took some skill to synchronize the paddles on the little craft, which glided effortlessly through the water when handled right. They were doing just fine until they reached the middle of the lake and Jo noticed a leak. Their tennis shoes were completely soaked.

"Hey, we've sprung a leak. We're going down!" she cried out. "Mayday! Mayday!"

"Calm down! Give me your bandanna!" Frannie yelled.

Jo unknotted the orange bandanna from her hair and waved it wildly overhead. Frannie grabbed the life jackets, handed one to Joleen, and put hers on. The water inside the canoe was ankle-deep, and rising.

"I guess we'll have to abandon ship," Frannie said. She squinted her eyes at the tiny figures moving around on the shore, but they were so far away it was impossible to tell who was who and what they were doing, much less if anyone noticed their distress signal. Just as both girls jumped overboard and were clinging to the side of their sinking canoe, they caught sight of an aluminum boat plowing toward them.

"Hey, what's up?" a deep voice called out after he cut the motor. As he drew close, Frannie recognized the lifeguard—the hero.

"We've got a leak!" Frannie yelled, forgetting that Joleen was supposed to do all the talking. Anyway, this was totally unplanned. Who would plan a silly scene like this—getting a leak in your canoe so you could hang off its side like a couple of drowned rats?

"Oh, yeah?" The blond lifeguard swung his lean brown legs over the side of his boat

70

and checked the sinking hull. "I can't see what's wrong. Hey, why don't you girls climb aboard? You look wet."

Frannie frowned. "No kidding."

"Nice to meet you, by the way. Have we met before?" He flashed Frannie a brilliant grin, his blue eyes filled with the same sparkling gold specks that danced on the water. "I'm Jim Wiseman, lifeguard and rescuer of beautiful damsels in distress."

A blush started up Frannie's neck. "That's a funny way to introduce yourself. I'm Frances Bronson—my friends call me Frannie, and" —she'd nearly forgotten poor Joleen—"my cousin, Joleen Windham."

"How do you do?" Jim extended a sun-browned hand to each girl, his hand lingering in Frannie's a moment longer. She quivered involuntarily at his touch. She noted that his straight, dark-blond hair and bleached eyebrows accentuated his rugged, tanned good looks, just as the bright-red lifeguard T-shirt set off his muscled body. His warm smile contrasted with the crisp command, "Let's get this baby into shore, shall we?" As his hand slid out of Frannie's, Joleen winked at her, and Frannie focused on her soggy shoes, feeling slightly ashamed. *Here I am going steady with a boy, and I'm caught flirting with the guy who's rescuing us from a sinking canoe!* she scolded herself.

Jim looped a nylon rope onto the canoe and hooked it up to his boat, then brought the engine to life and towed the canoe in. Frannie and Joleen perched up front, facing Jim. Frannie stared out across the water. That way, eyes averted, she could at least try to quiet the excitement simmering just beneath the surface each time she looked at Jim.

At the boat ramp, Jim helped Frannie and Joleen out of the boat and surveyed the damage to the canoe. "Looks like you ripped the canvas." He pointed out a long tear in the bottom. "I'm surprised you got all the way out to the middle of the lake." His broad shoulder muscles were taut as he secured his own craft, mesmerizing Frannie.

"So where's your car?" He turned abruptly to catch her wayward gaze.

Her face flushed bright red—oh, how she wished she could control that awful response! "Uh, Joleen's father's car is up there." She motioned vaguely.

"This way." Joleen took the lead. It was Frannie's turn to feel embarrassed.

Finally the boat was lashed onto her uncle's station wagon.

"Ready to go, then, huh?" Jim's cool blue eyes met Frannie's for a timeless moment.

"Thanks a lot," Frannie said.

"I just don't know what we would've done if you hadn't come along," Joleen said. Frannie whirled around in surprise—that was the most her cousin had ever said without coaching!

Jim laughed. "There's a strong possibility that you would've swum to shore and your little canoe would be at the bottom of the lake now."

"My uncle wouldn't be too happy about that," Frannie mumbled, unable to think of anything better to say.

Jim hung around for a minute longer, then finally said, "Well, I'd better shove off. I've got work to do, you know. There might be other pretty girls out there drowning."

Frannie laughed, feeling flattered. *What a funny guy,* she thought happily. *It isn't every day I meet a hero.*

"See you around."

"See you," she called, her knees turning to water as she watched him stride back down to the lifeguard tower.

"I don't know about me, but you certainly

do know how to make points," Joleen quipped.

Frannie had almost forgotten that Jo was standing beside her. Jo leaned against the car door, keys dangling casually from her fingers, a mile-wide grin on her face.

"Huh?" Frannie blinked, and Joleen burst into laughter.

# Chapter Eight

"Today's your day to order a hamburger," Frannie reminded Joleen as they dressed. She'd chosen a light blue skirt and flowered blouse and had even set her hair.

Joleen studied her with suspicion. "What's the occasion, Fran? Why did you do your hair differently? And why did you change the schedule? The next thing on the list was Band-Aids, wasn't it?"

"I told you we'd change the schedule around to suit you, and after our boat adventure, I thought it'd be better not to ask Jim for a Band-Aid today. Maybe you can do that tomorrow."

"You can't convince me, Frannie. I can see right through you."

"Oh, come on, Joleen, don't be ridiculous! I've got a boyfriend, remember?"

"That doesn't mean you can't have a roving eye." Joleen giggled triumphantly as she experimented with Frannie's mascara. "And I've got to say—he *is* cute."

"See you after work," Frannie muttered, leaving in a hurry so she wouldn't make her uncle late.

Her morning's work was cut out for her. Boxes of poster board had arrived late the day before, and she had to break them open and organize the brightly colored boards in their respective slots. It was a quiet morning, with few customers, so Frannie had plenty of time to mull over what her cousin had said earlier.

It was funny how she and Joleen had become close friends in such a short time. Jane, on the other hand, she didn't see much of—once in a while prancing along the beach with friends and at dinner every night. Sometimes her younger cousin consulted her on dress or makeup, but not often. Jane seemed to have her own ideas of what looked good, although to Frannie her color schemes were pretty loud. *Maybe I'm just too color-conscious,*

Frannie analyzed, *and Jo and I have similar tastes.*

Sharing a room with Joleen meant sharing more than simply living space. They were beginning to know each other well, and it wasn't surprising, really, that Jo had caught on to Frannie's fascination with Jim Wiseman. What girl in her right mind wouldn't find him attractive? Absently, Frannie wondered if those two people he'd saved last year were girls and if they'd fallen under his spell, too.

*Hey, I haven't fallen under his spell— yet,* she reprimanded herself. *He's good-looking, charming, but already I know he's not my type.* She had gone through all this with the Popularity Plan—she had discovered that the popular, sought-after boys were not the kind of guys she wanted. Jim obviously had to be another one of those.

*But,* an impish little voice inside her teased, *you haven't tried a lifeguard yet.*

Honestly, why had she fixed her hair, put on a skirt and blouse instead of jeans? She planned to change before going to the beach later, but she didn't usually get all fixed up unless she was excited about something . . . or someone.

"Yes, the young lady in the back can help you find what you want," she heard Mr. Preston say.

"You've got a customer."

Jim Wiseman, fully dressed in cords and a white T-shirt, appeared taller as he grinned down at her.

"Hi, Jim." Frannie straightened herself from her crouched position. "What can I help you with?"

"I need some stencils. I've got to paint a sign on the tower today."

"Sounds like fun," she mumbled, her lips going numb. *What's the matter with me?* she wondered, leading the way to the stencil sheets. "Here, take your pick."

"Thanks." He looked through them for a minute. Then as she turned to leave him to it, he said, "Oh, Frannie?"

"Yes?"

"You look really pretty today." His blue eyes shone with a look that just about melted her.

"Why, thank you," she replied demurely. "Anything else I can help you with?"

He winked. "Maybe later."

She hurried away, not wanting him to discover how much his presence affected her.

Her blood had started racing, making her woozy. She knelt down in front of the poster board, the rainbow colors swirling and blurring before her eyes. Frannie concentrated on getting the right colors in the right slots—which took an unnecessary amount of attention—until she heard the cash register total up Jim's purchases.

"See you, Frannie!" he called before stepping out the door.

She waved a weak goodbye, unaware that Mr. Preston was eyeing her with barely concealed amusement.

"So, you're ordering the hamburgers?" Frannie confronted Jo, who looked as if she were ready to back out.

"Is she? I can't believe it." Jane shook her head in surprise. "Order me a cheeseburger, fries, and a chocolate shake, please, Jo." Jane tossed her head with a self-confident air.

Frannie noted that Jo's green bikini showed off her deepening tan, and the freckles she wailed about incessantly had not spread like the plague as she insisted they would.

Like a person climbing the steps to the

guillotine, Joleen trudged up to the snack bar. Jane leaned over and whispered to Frannie, "My father will just die when he hears about this."

"She has to learn to do things herself. I know what it's like when you're really shy."

"You?" Jane was incredulous. "You've got nothing to be shy about."

"Neither does Joleen," Frannie reminded her. "People like us would give anything for an ounce of your self-confidence, Jane. You just don't know how lucky you are."

Suddenly Jane was on tiptoe, motioning toward the snack bar. "That's Jerry Ghio, the redhead. Isn't he cute? Now he's waiting on Joleen."

Beneath a froth of bright curls, Jerry's pleasant round face beamed as he belted out, "What'll ya have?" to the delight of the other workers.

Joleen cleared her throat and pronounced extra clearly, "Three cheeseburgers, one Pepsi, two chocolate shakes, and an order of fries," her voice quivering on the last word.

"Ya gonna eat it all yourself?" Jerry clowned.

Jane started to laugh, but Frannie clamped a hand over her mouth.

"No," shot back Jo.

"I didn't think so." He smiled at her, coaxing an unsure smile back.

"Then why'd you ask?" was her soft response.

"That doesn't sound like my sister!" Jane blurted from behind Frannie's palm.

The order successfully completed, the three girls walked down to the beach to eat. Jane ran off to join her friends, while Frannie praised Jo for her performance at the snack bar.

"Your comeback was great—I could never think of those wise remarks when I was doing the Plan. I stuttered more than anyone I know!"

Joleen laughed gaily. "If that's the truth, then you sure have changed, Frannie Bronson." She cast a longing glance at the crowd clustered around the lifeguard tower. Jim Wiseman was busy painting FIRST AID in big red stenciled letters on the first-aid box. Peter Culp sat surrounded by a group of pretty girls, with Sandi Sloan rubbing suntan lotion on his back.

Frannie watched Joleen's expression sag. "Look, as soon as he goes down to the water, you go down there, too," she suggested. "Maybe you can strike up a conversation. It might not be as hopeless as it looks. Remember, he noticed you when you caught the fish."

"I made a scene, that's why," she pointed out.

The opportunity came when six kids from the group strolled to the water's edge. Sandi dipped a daintily pointed toe into the water and twittered about its coldness. Peter plunged into the lake, his muscular arms slicing the water with clean strokes. Some of the other boys and girls followed his example. Jo looked hypnotized.

"Come on, Jo. Go in. Swim after him!" Frannie urged.

Joleen looked down at her long, slender legs, which were getting nicely tanned and losing their unsightly streaks. "Here goes nothing," she whispered, taking a deep breath.

*Bravo*, thought Frannie as Joleen inched her way into the water, then finally kicked off with a big splash. Frannie was near enough to hear Sandi's cutting remark: "What a klutz! She got my hair all wet, and now it's going to get all frizzy." She shrugged prettily. "Oh, well, there's a klutz in every crowd."

She got the laugh she tried for, along

with assurances that her hair always looked great.

But Sandi kept her eyes fastened on Peter's fast-moving form as he churned up to the buoy. Hardly a great swimmer with her windmill strokes, Joleen plowed alongside the others, but most of them were much faster swimmers and left her behind.

Sandi stiffened as she saw Joleen next to Peter at the buoy. From the beach it looked as if Jo was talking and laughing with the group. "Who is that girl?" Sandi asked.

"That's Joleen Windham—you know, Jane Windham's sister. The shy one," one of the other girls replied.

"She's a doll," a boy commented, and another whistled his agreement.

"Oh, Graham, you don't even know what a doll is. We'll have to give you some instruction, won't we, girls?"

Graham blushed, and the girls cracked up.

Surreptitiously, Frannie opened her notebook and wrote next to "possible snob"—"Suspicion confirmed."

The group snaked back to shore. A nice-looking brown-haired boy stood talking to Jo after the others walked up the beach. Frannie was dying to know who he was.

"That's the girl who caught the big trout the other day, remember?" Peter was telling Sandi, the admiration in his voice obvious.

"Is that the one?" Sandi smiled pertly. "You mean the klutz who fell off the pier, don't you?"

The others snickered, but Peter remained silent. At least he doesn't laugh at sick jokes, Frannie noted with relief.

"Guess what?" Joleen dripped water all over Frannie in her haste to spill her news. "That was Bob Wiseman—you know, Jim Wiseman's brother. I'm sure you haven't forgotten Jim." *Smart girl, how could I forget?* Frannie thought but said nothing. "He asked me if I could go to the dance tonight, Fran. Isn't that great?" Her eyes shone, and even with her hair hanging in strands, she looked beautiful. "I said I'd have to ask if it was all right, so he's going to call me and see!"

"That's wonderful!" Frannie cried. "Your first real date." Then she told her what had happened while Jo was talking to Bob.

"Peter said that, really?" She was awe-struck. All the way home she prompted Frannie to retell the story.

"Maybe it's not good for me to go out with another boy. What do you think?" Jo fretted.

"Go. You need the experience," Frannie advised. "And it won't hurt Peter to realize you're desirable—as long as you're just on a date, not together constantly."

Frannie was secretly more afraid of Joleen becoming known as a klutz, which would be an unfortunate tag for such a pretty girl. It was too bad Sandi had been so quick to latch onto the idea, plainly in hopes of making Joleen appear foolish. There had to be some way to keep that from happening, she decided.

There were two letters waiting for Frannie when she arrived at the house—one from her mother and one from Charlene.

She opened Charlene's letter first.

Dear Fran,

Everything's great here. Ronnie acts like a lost puppy without you, but it's good you're gone. I told you so. I bet you're having a ball. Patti & Bert broke up for a day but are back together. Jason's leaving for Idaho next weekend, so I'll be alone. Everything else the same. Write me.

Love,
Char

Dear Frannie,

I do hope you're being a good girl and helping your aunt and uncle. I worry about you catching cold—it is a different climate. Are you taking your vitamins? Your father came down with a dreadful cold Sunday, and I just know it's because he didn't take his Vitamin C. It's strange not having you here. Miss you.

Love,
Mom and Dad

Frannie felt a twinge of homesickness as she pictured her house without her in it. Her home had always seemed quiet in comparison with other more crowded households, so now it must seem like a museum with only two people living there.

While she, Joleen, and Jane got ready for the dance, the phone rang. "It sounds like that boyfriend of yours, Frannie," her aunt announced, her eyes twinkling with mischief. "I told him you were on your way out."

"You didn't!" gasped Frannie, quickly rehearsing what she would say to Ronnie. Would he understand?

"Don't worry, dear. It's good for a boy to realize you're not sitting around pining." Joyce Windham patted Frannie's shoulder. Since her aunt didn't know what was going on, she couldn't be blamed, Frannie thought, but she couldn't help resenting her interference.

"So, you're going out." Ronnie's words were a cold accusation.

"Yes. Ronnie, I'm going to a small dance with my cousins. Jane is only thirteen and can't go without an older person," she explained. "Joleen is going with a date."

"Are you planning on dancing with anyone?" he asked.

"I don't know. I mean, I never thought about it."

"You're going to a dance, and you never thought about dancing?"

*Boy, am I in trouble!* Frannie's mind whirled frantically. "Look, Ronnie, I've been at the beach, and I've been working. I'm going to the dance for something to do. Is there anything wrong with that?"

"It sounds like you've been doing enough already."

"What is that supposed to mean?" she demanded, her anger rising.

"Here you're supposed to be my girl, and you're running around all over the beach all day and dancing at night. How do I know you haven't got a date, too?"

"I don't have a date, and I know I'm your girl, Ronnie. But I'm not going to sit around this house moping over you all summer when I could be out doing things."

"We have dances here. We have beaches, so what's the attraction up *there*?" he grumbled.

"It's different here, Ronnie. The scenery's different, and so are the people." An uninvited image of Jim Wiseman appeared, but she quickly brushed it aside. "It's an experience, I thought you understood all that."

"What am I supposed to understand?" he shouted, and Frannie held the receiver away from her ear. "Here's my girl running around, maybe with some other guy, while I'm sitting here with nothing to do."

"That's not my fault, Ronnie!" she retorted. "I'm not going out with any boys, I promise you!"

"That's an easy promise to make, since you're two hundred miles away," he shot back. "Anyway, don't forget—I'm quite aware of your ability to attract guys."

"You're not being fair, Ronnie," she protested. "I've been working on Joleen. Tonight Joleen has her first date."

"So you're going along to make sure everything turns out all right?" he said sarcastically.

Suddenly she wondered if she even *liked* him. Her stomach was in a wild turmoil. "This is long distance, Ronnie. I just wonder if you want to spend your money on this argument," she suggested coolly.

"You've got a point, Frances. Goodbye." And he hung up.

Frannie was trembling. He never, ever called her Frances.

# Chapter Nine

Joleen looked radiant in an accordion-pleated lime-green dress with spaghetti straps, and it was obvious Bob thought so, too, as he swept her out of the house and into his battered Volkswagen.

"I hope that that car isn't any indication of the way he drives," Joleen's father said, frowning as Bob started the noisy engine.

"Don't you worry, Mort, our Joleen knows how to take care of herself. She's got a good head on her shoulders and wouldn't pick an unsuitable boy to go out with."

Frannie's uncle had allowed her to use his car for the occasion, so he spent a few minutes familiarizing her with the lights before she and Jane left.

"I can't believe my parents are letting me go to this dance," Jane said excitedly. "If it wasn't for you, I wouldn't be going, you know."

Frannie listened halfheartedly to her chatter, thinking back over her conversation—or rather, argument—with Ronnie. Who did he think he was, trying to dictate what she would do with herself two hundred miles away? Did he really expect her to sit in her aunt's house and dream about him? He wouldn't do the same thing if the situation were reversed. Or would he?

A combination of guilt and anger tore at her, unsettling her scarcely eaten dinner. She wished she could yank back some of her angry words, make things all right between them, even though she felt completely justified in saying what she had. Ronnie acted like such a creep. For a moment, she even wondered what it was she had liked about him in the first place.

A row of bobbing Japanese paper lanterns designated the Canteen, a log house converted into a recreation room for both tourists and locals. Music wafted out to greet them, and through an open doorway they could glimpse the swaying couples.

"Ooh, I can't wait! I wonder who's going

to be here!" Jane could hardly contain herself until Frannie had the car parked.

"I'm sure you'll see everyone you know." Frannie smiled, knowing that Jane and her friends emulated whatever the older, popular crowd was doing. She guessed that was the way it was in her junior-high days, though she wasn't popular then, so she didn't watch so closely.

The moment they got to the door, Jane disappeared into the crowd. Frannie stood on tiptoe to see where Joleen and Bob were and spotted them next to the punch bowl. In her one-and-a-half inch heels, Jo was about a half-inch taller than Bob, and Frannie noticed him attempting to stand straighter to compensate for the difference.

Then she looked for Peter Culp. Joleen would want to know all there was to know about him. She could have told Ronnie she was going to the dance as a spy—that would have got to him. But, she fumed, any excuse she might have given wouldn't have satisfied his jealousy, for that was all it was, she felt certain.

Peter and Sandi were slow-dancing off in one corner, Sandi's golden head nestled against his shoulder. Frannie hoped Jo didn't see, though it was inevitable that she'd see them together eventually.

"Frannie."

Whirling around, she came face-to-face with Jim Wiseman.

"Do you want to dance?" he asked.

She nodded, slipping into his arms, vaguely recalling Ronnie's protests about her dancing. She could promise not to date, but not to *dance*? That was really crazy, she thought, Jim's arms tightening about her waist.

"You look nice," Jim told her.

"Thanks." The compliment lifted her spirits. She'd worn the outfit at home a lot—a full white skirt with red top and gold jewelry, but Ronnie had never commented on it. "Do you compliment all the girls like that?" she teased.

"No. Only the best-looking ones," he quipped, and she laughed, delighted, thinking how relaxed and easygoing he seemed, so different from Ronnie.

He spun her around, and feeling slightly dizzy, she could have been dancing on air. Frannie felt free, uninhibited by the feelings that usually weighed her down when she was dancing with Ronnie. She usually worried if Ronnie was having a good time, if she was boring him, or if he wanted to go home, instead of just being with him, enjoying the dance, as she was now.

The theme song to "The Greatest American Hero" filled the room, and Frannie and Jim really got into it. Jim was a good dancer, something Ronnie was not.

"I feel like I'm dancing on air," Frannie confessed.

"Oh, yeah? Because of me?" He laughed and grabbed her fingers. A hot rush sped up her arm, and she pulled her hand away as if she'd gotten a shock.

"Oh, no!" she began to protest, but amusement played in Jim's eyes at her response, and she felt sure he wouldn't take anything she said seriously.

After a few dances, Jim suggested a walk in the woods to cool off. *What would Ronnie think about that?* Frannie wondered briefly, before pushing the thought out of her mind. She wanted to have fun, just as she'd told him earlier—even if she did feel a little too daring stepping outside the Canteen with Jim.

She could hear the gentle lap of the lake against the sand, the muted sounds of laughter and music, the soft rustle of pine needles beneath their feet. Jim casually slipped an arm over her shoulders when she shivered.

Ronnie hardly ever did things like that, Frannie thought guiltily. He cared about her— she was sure of it—but he was always hold- ing back, stopping himself from doing the little things that showed he cared. Sometimes, Frannie knew, he really *wanted* to hold her hand when she was frightened or stroke her hair when she was depressed, but he couldn't; for some reason. Even his kisses, and they had done their share of kissing, were not always terribly passionate.

Maybe it was because Ronnie was still shy. Or maybe he was afraid to lose her, so he pretended he didn't care too much. Then he wouldn't hurt later if he did lose her. But, thought Frannie practically, you couldn't go through life holding back. And besides, he was losing her just as surely with his odd behavior as he would any other way.

"I'm going to Humboldt State to study forestry," Jim told Frannie, and she snapped back to reality. "I figure it's good to get away from home. I've lived here all my life, and I'll probably spend most of my life in places like this, especially if I go into forestry."

Frannie admired the strong profile out- lined against the dark filigree of leaves. "I know how you feel—that's why I decided to stay up here for the summer. A change of scenery. I'll probably major in art." She almost mentioned Ronnie also majoring in art but quickly figured Ronnie had no place in this conversation, even if he was so much on her mind.

They talked about places they dreamed of someday seeing, of activities they both enjoyed, and their jobs. Amazing, Frannie reflected, that when you talked to someone like this, a gap started closing as a few little bridges of interest were hastily built between you. When you knew someone really well, as she knew Ronnie, you were linked up in so many ways you could almost cross the bridges blindfolded. Funny, Frannie thought, how building a relationship was the same but different with every person you met. It was always a process of closing the gaps, but *how* you closed the gaps was what made friendships fun and interesting. The gaps couldn't ever be completely closed, could they? Could you ever know a person so thoroughly? Maybe that was what was happening between her and Ronnie. But, no, they hadn't known each other long enough. Or maybe they had stopped trying to bridge the gaps. It was all so complicated. . . .

"Did you really save those two people last summer?" Frannie asked suddenly.

"Yeah, why?" Jim's expression grew serious.

"Joleen and Jane mentioned it, so I just wondered, that's all," she replied quickly, not wanting to press him further if he didn't want to talk about it.

His eyes grew distant, focused on some vague point across the lake. "Two girls swam out to the buoy, and one got a cramp and couldn't make it back in. The other girl was only about eight and couldn't support the cramped one, and she started to go under, too, so I jumped in and did my hero thing." He shrugged it off. "All in a day's work."

"A real hero," she remarked with obvious admiration. If only Ronnie—*no*. It wasn't fair to compare Ronnie and Jim all the time; not fair to either of them.

He turned her to face him, then lifted her chin until her gaze met his. "Am I your hero?"

Fear filled her throat. He was moving too fast. "I—I don't know, Jim. I hear you're a hero to the beach crowd," she murmured, purposely evasive. *I'm not being fair to Ronnie, not being fair to Ronnie.*

"But not to you, huh?" He looked and sounded disappointed. "Listen, I'd like to take you out sometime, Frannie."

She shifted her focus to a squirrel scampering up a tree trunk. "I don't know . . . . I mean, I'll have to see."

He raked tanned fingers through his hair and bit his lower lip in a thoughtful pose. Frannie wished she could escape from this somehow. She wanted to go out with him, didn't she? Then, why not? He was certainly tempting, and she'd been dating Ronnie for so long she didn't know what it would be like with another boy. And, she thought, she had to be fair to herself, as well as to Ronnie and Jim.

"If you mean you have to ask your aunt and uncle, I understand that. But if you mean you don't want to . . ." His blue eyes penetrated her own, and she quivered inside.

"It's not that, Jim. I really want to, but I have to think about it, OK?" She should tell him about Ronnie, she thought. She should be honest with him. He'd been only nice to her so far.

Jim whispered "OK" into her hair, his breath raising goosebumps along her skin.

And then he drew her to him and gently kissed her.

Fire raced through her veins at his touch. Frannie wanted his kisses, his hands stroking her as if he were making a new discovery, but when he locked her in an even tighter embrace, she broke away.

"We ought to get back to the dance," she whispered. "Jane and Joleen will be looking for me."

"Jane and Joleen will be busy," he mumbled, his face in her hair.

Frannie pushed him away with more force. "I said I'd better go, Jim. Come on." She slipped her hand through his, and although he was reluctant, he followed her back to the Canteen.

*Ronnie was right about me,* she thought. *I'm just barely keeping my promise. But I am keeping it. That should tell us both something.*

# Chapter Ten

Frannie had Saturday off, and Mr. and Mrs. Windham insisted the girls take a horseback ride onto Pine Ridge with them. After a huge breakfast, they drove up to the stable.

Mort Windham made the mistake of telling the guide Joleen had ridden before, referring, Joleen explained later, to the pony she'd ridden at the county fair exactly three times. So, Joleen was given Tex, the most spirited horse.

From the beginning of their ride, Joleen had trouble controlling Tex. Suddenly, while Mr. and Mrs. Windham argued over the name of some wild berries they'd seen, Jo's horse spun around in mid-trail and galloped back the way he'd come, along the rocky trail complicated by dangerously low, overhanging branches.

"Hey, Mom, Dad! *Do something*!" shouted Jane, flapping her reins in the air.

Frannie reined her horse around and kicked her until she began to canter. Jockey-style, she clung to the horse's back to avoid being swept off by the branches.

Finally she saw Jo's horse grazing at the bottom of the hill—minus Jo.

"Joleen!" she called.

"I'm here." An arm with a torn long sleeve waved from below a gnarled pine tree. "I guess old Tex just wanted me off. Another one of Mom and Dad's fantastic ideas," she grumbled.

The guide, a cute, sunburned boy in a cowboy hat, galloped over to see if Jo was all right. "Tex will find his way back," he assured her.

The girls giggled. Who would worry about Tex? He seemed to know exactly what he was doing!

"I can't do anything without getting in a mess," Jo complained later as she changed into her swimsuit and discovered a red gash along her thigh. "I mean, here I get over the orange streaks, and now I'm injured. I'm so dumb."

"Just lie on the side with the cut," counseled Frannie. "Anyway, if someone does notice it, consider it a conversation piece."

"Ha-ha. I feel stupid even going to the beach today, Fran—after last night." She sighed heavily. "Peter doesn't know I'm alive."

"If he didn't know you were alive, why did he ask you to dance?" Peter had asked Jo to slow-dance, just once, but it was enough to turn Sandi Sloan's complexion a light shade of green.

"Compared to Sandi, I might as well be a fly on the wall."

They kept talking about it all the way down to the beach. Frannie had brought her stationery, and she started a letter to Ronnie while Joleen shuffled over to the lifeguard tower to ask Jim for a Band-Aid. Frannie simply pretended she didn't know what Jo was doing, because Jim would probably think Frannie had sent her cousin over there as a spy—especially after last night.

But far worse was the fact that Frannie couldn't think of anything to say to Ronnie. She was still angry with him, and now guilt overlaid her anger, complicating all her feelings. Then, thinking of Jim, her doubts and yearnings began all over again.

Mentally Frannie started a mean note to Ronnie:

> Dear Ronald,
>     I am on a gorgeous, sun-drenched beach, in a skimpy bikini, surrounded by cute boys. . . .

But she would never do that to him. She tried again, this time more seriously, actually taking pen to paper.

> Dear Ronnie,
>     I've been thinking over our argument last night, and I want to apologize.

No, that was wrong. Why should she apologize? She hadn't really done anything wrong—had she?

Frannie started the letter three times and tore each one up in disgust. On the brink of tears, she realized she was not ready to speak to Ronnie yet.

Sandi Sloan flitted down to the water's edge with Peter not far behind. She scooped a paper cupful of water and flung it at him, giggling in delight as he wiped his face. But she was unprepared when he cupped his hand in the lake and dashed water at her.

"Oh, Pete, you messed up my hair!" she said, pouting, shaking the droplets out of her glossy curls. She looked ready to cry, and Peter rushed over to soothe her. Sandi looked up at him, blinking and forcing a smile, and Peter ate it up. Frannie glanced over at the tower to see Joleen standing with Chip Daniels, watching the whole scene.

"Did you get the Band-Aid?" Frannie asked when Jo flopped down on her towel.

"No, he was out." Joleen looked wistfully at Peter. "Tomorrow the group is going for a picnic to the other side of the lake, and Chip asked if I'd like to go."

"Well, *go!*" urged Frannie. "Maybe you'll get an opportunity to talk to Peter then."

Joleen seemed very glum about her prospects but was bright and cheerful Sunday morning when Chip came to pick her up. Frannie was just putting stamps on two letters, one to her parents and the other to Charlene—she hadn't been able to write to Ronnie—when the doorbell rang.

"Hi." Jim Wiseman grinned sheepishly, as if he weren't sure what Frannie's response would be.

"Hi, Jim," she said, butterflies leaping in her stomach at the sight of him, in a way they certainly no longer did at the sight of Ronnie.

"I was wondering if you'd like to go on a picnic with me and some of the others. I know Joleen's going, and I've got the day off."

"I'll see," Frannie said and went to find her aunt. There was no reason in the world why she shouldn't go out on the boat with Jim, was there? After all, it wasn't a date or anything, just a group of kids going out for the day. She wouldn't be breaking her promise to Ronnie—yet.

Frannie's aunt wanted to make a lunch, but Jim said he'd already fixed one and there was no need. Frannie quickly jumped into a bathing suit, grabbed a towel, and they left.

Once they were wedged into the boat like sardines, Frannie felt better. It did not seem as if she was *with* Jim exclusively, as she'd halfway hoped. In the next boat, Peter Culp led the group in singing "One Hundred Bottles of Beer on the Wall."

Poor Joleen was crammed between Chip and Sandi!

When the two boats reached the cove where they would be picnicking, Peter suggested a swim. "Let's race before lunch," he announced. "The winner can have my choco-late cupcakes."

"Count me out," said Sandi, patting her scarf-protected curls.

Joleen lined up next to Chip, and Peter glanced at her appraisingly. Wendy Collins, a tiny brunette in a one-piece red suit, was the judge. Ten swimmers plunged into the water when she shouted "Go!" and made a beeline for a whale-shaped rock, which they had to touch before swimming back to shore.

No one could keep up with Jim, who was far and away the best swimmer of all. After nearly everyone had reached the shore, Frannie said teasingly, "It's a relief to know that our lifeguard is also the best swimmer among us."

Jim didn't answer. "Hey, who's that out there?" he yelled sharply, pointing out a pair of arms flailing halfway between the rock and shore.

Without hesitation he dove in, swimming underwater nearly all the way. As the dark head of the swimmer broke the surface, Frannie's heart sank. Joleen.

Expertly, Jim brought her safely to shore. She was coughing and spluttering, her face red with exertion.

"Oh, no, *her again.*" Sandi sighed, hitting her forehead. "Some people will do *anything* for attention!" The laughter that followed broke the tension, just as it shifted the spotlight back to Sandi, where she wanted it.

Meanwhile, Frannie draped a towel around her shivering cousin's shoulders. "What happened?" she asked Jo, but she couldn't stop coughing to answer.

"It seems she swallowed water, and it went down the wrong pipe," Jim explained. "You know, it could happen to anybody." He shot a glance at Sandi, who looked smugly pretty in her matching pink-flowered cover-up.

Sandi shrugged prettily. "It happens to some *anybodies* a little too often, doesn't it!" She darted a meaningful glance at Jo.

"Hey, are you OK?" Peter asked Joleen, who looked like a drowned rat. She nodded silently.

Frannie's heart ached for her.

"It could happen to anyone, really," Peter echoed, trying to reassure her.

"Anyone clumsy enough to swallow water instead of air," Sandi added, giving a superior smirk.

"Why don't you just shut up?" Frannie retorted.

"Yeah." One of the other girls giggled. "Some people are afraid just to get wet." Wendy Collins broke up at that remark, but not before Frannie saw the storm gathering on Sandi's face.

Sandi snatched up her towel and angrily walked away. Plainly, Sandi Sloan wasn't used to being told off, but Frannie suspected that wasn't all that bugged her. It appeared that Sandi wanted Joleen out of the picture. Frannie wasn't sure, yet, whether Sandi was downgrading Jo because she wanted the other kids to dislike Jo or because Peter had showed too much interest in Jo for Sandi's liking.

Still, Jo didn't need a reputation as a klutz, for then she'd be considered a joke. What she needed was a great *image*, and, being the daughter of an ad man, Frannie knew all about images. Everyone had a potential image, according to her father, although very often it was hidden and had to be drawn out for others to see.

*So what can we do with Jo that will make her unforgettable?* she pondered, offering her cousin a somewhat squished tuna sandwich. She isn't sports-minded—God forbid!

—she has a great stamp collection, but what is really *special* about her? There must be something—something that will make everyone at the beach notice her, knock Peter Culp entirely off his feet, and shut Sandi Sloan's big mouth once and for always.

For the life of her, Frannie didn't know what it would be.

## Chapter Eleven

"I'll never go down on that beach again!" Joleen sobbed into her pillow, her hair fanning across it like a dark crescent. "Did you hear what she said about me?"

"Of course I heard. She's just jealous, Jo. Otherwise, why would she even bother putting you down publicly?" Frannie reasoned, for she couldn't honestly think of another reason for the verbal attack. Jo hadn't done anything to Sandi. "I think the other kids took your side, anyway," she added. "Nobody likes being called a klutz, and everybody's klutzy sometimes."

"I don't care what you say, Frannie. I'm going into hiding. No one will see me for at least two weeks, and by that time they will have forgotten about me!"

Joleen's face was red and blotchy when she raised it from her pillow.

"You've made so much progress, Jo. It'd be a shame to quit now. People are just getting to know who you are," Frannie insisted.

Joleen moped around the house for exactly twenty-four hours, until Jerry Ghio, the snack-bar attendant, called up and asked her for a date. There was a momentary flutter over whether or not she should go, and "Will Peter think I like Jerry?" Then, with Frannie's encouragement, she finally accepted.

Frannie received a letter from Ronnie, which might as well have been lifted right off his calendar—a list of the week's events. There was no mention of their argument the other night, as if it had never taken place. How could he ignore it?

"How romantic. A letter from Ronnie!" Jo batted her eyelashes at her reflection in the mirror.

"Yeah, really romantic—if you can call the volleyball tournament at the beach and spilled popcorn romantic," grumbled Frannie.

"Huh?"

"Read it." Frannie slapped the letter down in front of her cousin, who read it eagerly, having never received a letter from a boy in her life.

"He sounds like he's holding back, Fran," Joleen told her, pushing a silk flower into her hair.

"What do you mean? It's just a list of activities, for goodness' sake," Frannie snapped. After all, Ronnie had been so possessive the other day, as though he owned her. Now he was just trying to brush over their argument, as if it were of no importance.

"No, that's just a cover, I bet. He's lonely without you, and he's scared to tell you so. Here. Listen to these last lines.

'The town is sure quiet this summer. Mostly I just go back and forth between the T-shirt factory and the beach. Almost everyone is away right now. I think I'll be glad to go off to San Francisco in September—but I hope I get to see you first.'

"See? He knows you're having a super time, and it hurts," she said.

"Ha!" Frannie scoffed, but deep down she

knew with Ronnie, holding back was the name of the game.

After Jo sailed off, leaving a fragrant trail of her favorite Jungle Gardenia lingering in the room, the telephone rang. It was Jim Wiseman.

"I know this is short notice, Frannie, but can you go for a ride tonight? We can be back early, since we've both got to work tomorrow."

The idea sounded nice, Frannie mused, and Jim was so willing to please her. The cloud Ronnie's letter had cast dissipated a little. It was a beautiful night for a ride. And a ride wasn't a date . . . exactly. Frannie accepted, pushing back the niggling voice that warned her not to. *I'm on vacation,* she told it, *and I ought to be able to do what I want. Besides, Ronnie never has to know.*

The roar of Jim's little yellow sports car reverberated through the silent woods as the wind rushed through Frannie's hair like giant fingers. It was exhilarating and completely washed away the heavy thoughts she'd had earlier.

Jim parked the car in a wooded cul-de-sac that overlooked the mountains, the trees darkly silhouetted against a royal-blue sky, stars crusting the heavens like rock salt. Frannie and Ronnie hadn't been anywhere this romantic in months.

"You know, after this summer we probably won't see each other again," Jim said softly.

He rested his arm on the back of the seat. "Maybe we'll run into each other someday," Frannie said, smiling nervously.

"Do you have a boyfriend back home?" he asked.

She turned to him, so astonished by his perception that she couldn't answer readily.

"I mean, you seem so distant, like you're thinking of somebody else when you're with me," Jim went on. "I can understand that, Frannie, but I'm really crazy about you."

He leaned closer to kiss her, but she turned her face away from his lips. "I do have a boyfriend back home, but we aren't getting along very well." *What a cop-out*, she thought, hating herself for saying that. She hadn't meant to talk to anyone about it, least of all Jim, but here it came burbling out. "We've been going together a long time. Ronnie and I are—changing."

"I know what you mean," Jim said sympathetically. "Love has to be fresh, spontaneous. Some couples get like old married people."

*Old married people*—was that what she and Ronnie had become? They knew exactly how each other felt most of the time, their weekends were entirely predictable, there were no surprises left.

She didn't tell Jim that Ronnie was annoyed with her for taking off and not sharing those dull weekends with him—well, they weren't all dull, Frannie had to admit. There were times when Ronnie could be very romantic, but those times were fewer and farther between than when they'd first started going together.

A sudden pang of longing for Ronnie pierced Frannie just as Jim pulled her to him and kissed her. Her pulse leaped at his touch, but suddenly she felt frightened of his intensity and tried to draw back. But he held her in a viselike grip, caressing her face, her hair, her lips. . . . She was violently drawn to his animal magnetism yet she shrank back with a strange mixture of emotions—guilt, fear, and something she couldn't quite put her finger on. Was it, she wondered, herself that she was afraid of?

Or *was* it fear? Suddenly, Frannie thought, she *missed* Ronnie. Their weekends together might be predictable, but they were comfortable and safe—and dear because they were Ronnie. *Oh, Ronnie, I don't know how I feel anymore.*

"It's getting late," she whispered, pushing at him. "Remember, we've both got to work tomorrow."

Reluctantly he let her go but held her close against him as they drove home. They talked about school and their plans, and every so often he would murmur a compliment or squeeze her shoulder affectionately. She closed her eyes and remembered how it was with Ronnie in the beginning—how every time he touched her, her skin would ripple. How she didn't want to wash her hand after he held it, how she dreamed of his lips on hers. Being together had seemed so right, so perfect. They fit together exactly—his arms around her felt completely natural, and she didn't even have to stand on tiptoe to kiss him good night.

As she thought of them, the way they were—in the past tense—tears filled her eyes and silently spilled into her lap. Was it gone forever? Or could she go back to him now and have it all again?

\*      \*      \*

A week later Frannie's father called. He was so excited that he didn't even ask how she was. "You remember how long I've wanted to get the Kay Nugent jeans account?" he asked, then went on without waiting for her to answer. "Well, the word is out that they're dissatisfied with their current agency and are looking for a new one. I've already submitted a proposal, and I'm going to make a test commercial for them to try and get the account. I've got this great idea, and I need an all-American girl. So naturally I thought of you."

"Oh, Dad, you know how I hate being in front of a camera," she protested. Her dad and his crazy business! The last time she'd done a commercial for him she was a dancing milk carton for a milk advisory board. Her friends thought she was hilarious.

"Don't be shy, Fran. You'd be perfect. Also, I want to shoot at Cherry Lake. The setting's fabulous . . ." he went on, oblivious to Frannie's sputtered complaints.

"Just a minute, Dad." She got a sudden, crazy idea. "How about using Joleen? She's tall, pretty—she'd be *perfect*! You don't care if the girl's a blond or brunette, do you?"

"Well, no—she is a pretty girl, and she photographs nicely." Her father sounded thoughtful. "Yes. Would Joleen be willing to do it?"

"Of course!" Frannie clinched the decision with more confidence than she actually felt, but this was the very thing Joleen needed to bring her out of her shell. "Joleen would love to do it."

Joleen entered the room at that moment and eyed her cousin warily. "Just what would I love to do?" she demanded.

Frannie couldn't contain her giggles. "Wait until I tell you!"

# Chapter Twelve

The Popularity Plan, set in motion by Frannie and Jo, was now in full swing and operating largely under its own steam. Frannie insisted that they carry it out for a third week, just to insure its success. Jo complained that she'd already gone on three dates, which was more than she'd had in her entire life, so why push her luck?

"Exposure is the name of the game," Frannie insisted.

They were down at the beach the next afternoon with the boat, pretending to be unable to start the outboard. They had tried this plan a week before, but an elderly man had come to their aid. This time Chip Daniels jogged down from the bait shop to give a hand, and within seconds the motor roared to life.

Joleen looked stunned by the sudden noise. Frannie elbowed her until she smiled at Chip.

"Gee, thanks, Chip. I don't know what we would've done without you."

Chip blushed at the compliment, curling his toes into his sandal uppers. "Aw, you're welcome. It was nothing." He glanced at Frannie as though he'd prefer that she disappear, so she took the hint.

"I'm going to see if Jim has a Band-Aid," she told Jo and skipped off toward the tower. That simple encounter ended with Chip asking Jo to the dance the following Friday night.

Wednesday's plan was for Jo to buy something from Peter's father's shop, which was probably the hardest thing in the world for her to do. "I mean, it's so obvious," she wailed, hiding her face in her hands while they stood across the street, safely out of sight as Frannie gave her a pep talk.

"Well, you could go in there with a stocking over your head so he wouldn't know who you are—but then, he might get the wrong impression," she said, teasing. But one look at Jo's wan face told her she wasn't in a joking mood. "It's a chance to speak to him alone, Jo, without Ms. Sloan around to mess things up. He's a nice guy, and if he doesn't get all her static, he can see you for what you really are."

Joleen wasn't sure what she really was, but bravely she crossed the street, bought the prearranged jogging shorts, and carried them to the counter.

Frannie watched the two talking, Peter laughing at something Jo said, Jo's head inclined to one side, her ponytail draped over her shoulder. He brushed hair out of his eyes, rang up the purchase, they talked a little more, and finally, Jo ran out to meet Frannie, clutching the bag to her chest.

Breathlessly, she related what had happened. "It was a great conversation! He said these were the best jogging shorts they had, and did I run a lot, and I said, no, but I was going to, and plus I'd outgrown my other ones, and he laughed and looked at my legs, and said, 'Oh, yeah? I know you didn't outgrow them sideways, because you're just the right size,' and I nearly melted. And then he asked me if I'd be at the beach later, and I said yes, and he said, 'Then I'll see you there!' " She stopped to take a deep breath, sea-green

121

eyes shining, her face flushed and tanned and perfect for a commercial, thought Frannie. The flush of first love.

"So what do you think, Frannie? Is he inviting me to the beach, or is he going to sit with me, maybe? What does it mean?"

"It could mean he's going to look for you at the beach, or maybe he expects to sit with you and talk some more," Frannie said, guessing, because it was hard to know a boy's intentions.

Joleen prepared a picnic lunch and waited for Peter to make an appearance at the beach, but Sandi Sloan got to him first and invited him to share her towel. Frannie noticed him casting occasional glances at Joleen, but it was obvious he was stuck with Sandi. Yet Joleen was not consoled by his glances and didn't eat a bite of her carefully packed lunch.

Thursday, Frannie had Joleen order hamburgers from Jerry again. Jim and Peter were sitting in the tower, and Jim casually suggested that the four of them eat together. They exchanged small talk—Peter's boat, Jim's lifeguarding, a television program Peter and Jim had seen. But to see the joy on Joleen's face, you would think they were discussing issues of major importance.

"Oh, by the way," Frannie put in slyly, unable to miss this opportunity for advertisement, "Joleen's going to appear in a test commercial that my father is filming up here."

Peter's dark eyes fastened on Jo, causing two bright spots to appear on her cheeks. "Is that so? What kind of commercial?"

"Jeans," was all Jo was able to manage.

"Kay Nugent jeans," Frannie added. "They'll be shooting Saturday."

"Wow! Let me know when, will you, Jo?" Peter asked softly.

Jo nodded and whispered, "I will." She and Peter gazed into each other's eyes so intently that Frannie and Jim might as well have been nonexistent.

Friday was spent getting ready for the Bronsons. Joleen had a date that evening with Chip, which she wished she didn't have to keep now that Peter had spoken to her. Frannie decided that any other plan ideas could be postponed until the next week, which was a relief to Joleen.

When Mr. and Mrs. Bronson arrived, the Windhams made their usual huge to-do. Mort Windham put some hefty steaks onto the grill. Mrs. Windham had made two huge salads, garlic bread, and a chocolate cake, and afterward everyone happily complained of being stuffed.

Jane pouted because she hadn't been chosen to model the jeans. They were beautiful jeans, jeans any girl would love to own. Kay Nugent was scrawled in the designer's handwriting across the hip pocket, with a bird in flight stitched just below the signature. The jeans were stitched with light-blue thread instead of orange or yellow. Joleen looked perfect in them.

"With this red silk blouse, you'll be absolutely stunning," Mrs. Bronson said, holding the blouse up to Joleen. The color suited Jo, almost matching the excited flush in her cheeks.

The next morning Frannie fixed Jo's hair, combing out a rich tumble of curls from the rollers she'd slept on that night. Then she helped her put on makeup, while her father and the cameramen hiked around the lake, looking for the ideal place to shoot.

By the time Jo was ready, Mr. Bronson had accumulated a trail of excited kids and teens who wanted to watch the filming, hoping to get in on "Hollywood." Frannie tried to tell them that this was not for Hollywood, but a test commercial. They remained an avid audience.

As the crowd grew larger, Frannie became aware that Joleen was attracting a lot of attention—especially from the guys.

"Hey, Joleen, you look great!" Chip Daniels yelled at her, grinning his appreciation.

"Hey, where've you been all my life, gorgeous?" Jason Wentworth shouted, which brought a ripple of applause.

Jim strolled over to stand with Frannie, but even his eyes followed Joleen as she graciously accepted her audience's acclaim, blushing prettily.

Frannie wondered what Ronnie would say to her if she were in Jo's shoes. He so rarely noticed her in a special way anymore. Didn't he realize that other boys thought she was pretty? she wondered, thinking of all that had happened since she'd left home. Was he taking her for granted? Or, again, was he just holding back, too shy to venture forth with a compliment? Probably the latter, but, Frannie decided, that was going to have to change. She and Ronnie would have to have a talk about it—and soon.

Within an alcove of trees, bordered on one side by the shimmering, glassy lake,

Joleen stood in front of a camera, radiant in her fire-engine-red blouse and the jeans, which were cinched in at the waist by a gold chain belt. She had on a pair of navy wedge-heeled sandals that made her even taller—*just like a real model*, thought Frannie excitedly.

Out of the corner of her eye she saw Peter at the front of the crowd, not missing a thing. Frannie went over to him. "Isn't she beautiful?" she prompted.

He glanced at Frannie absently. "Oh, yeah, she's terrific! She ought to be a model or something, you know? Like that Brooke Shields."

A few whistles pierced the cool morning air as the shooting began. A very gentle chestnut-brown mare had been brought onto the set. Jo was to ride onto the scene and dismount in front of the camera. Remembering the day Jo had been thrown from her horse, Frannie felt nervous and worried. But Jo handled the horse beautifully.

"What a doll!" a boy standing next to Frannie said as Jo galloped between the trees, hair flying, the full sleeves of the blouse shining in the sunlight. If not for the contemporary jeans, she could have been a medieval heroine.

They did several takes and then Mr. Bronson asked for a boy from the audience. "How about you?" Frannie said to Peter, who promptly turned crimson. "Listen, I know a lot about doing commercials, and I think you'd be perfect for this shot."

Frannie didn't know if Peter believed her or not, but nevertheless, he strode out to where Jo sat on the horse and listened patiently to the instructions to help her dismount this time when she rode onto the set.

Peter looked great in a light-brown sweater and checked shirt. As he reached for the horse's bridle to steady her, holding his hand out to Joleen, their eyes met and didn't waver. Joleen floated from the saddle, and Peter's hand dropped to her waist.

The camerman went wild. "Let's take more," he cried. "These two have *some* chemistry."

The shooting went so perfectly, Frannie thought she was watching a dream, and Joleen obviously was living one.

"Ever since you got here, Frannie, Joleen has been really unbelievable," Jim said, watching the production thoughtfully. "Last year she was in my trig class, and I never heard a sound from her all year long. She never talked to anyone. Now look at her! She's like a different girl."

"I guess you could say that," murmured Frannie, suppressing an urge to smile.

Peter walked over to Jim and Frannie after the filming.

"Hey, Jim, I wondered if you and—"

Whatever he was going to ask was cut off by Sandi Sloan's appearance. She slipped her dainty, braceleted arm through Peter's, batting her silky lashes at him. "Peter, could I talk to you for a minute?" she said in a hushed, throaty voice.

Peter turned several shades of red before replying, "Uh, sure."

They wove through the crowd, Sandi leading the way. A few minutes later, while Frannie was trying to get to Joleen, she was alarmed to hear Sandi's voice rising above the hubbub: "You've made a fool of me, Peter, and I just won't stand for it. I hate you!"

With an angry toss of her head, she stormed toward the parking lot. Peter looked as if he wanted to crawl under a rock.

"Poor Pete," Jim commiserated. "That Sandi's a real pain."

"If that's so, it sure took him a long time to find out," Frannie said, shaking her head.

At the same time, she knew that when you really care for someone, you overlook a lot of his faults. That was certainly true of Ronnie and herself.

Though sorry for Peter, Frannie was pleased with the outcome. As Sandi's outraged figure disappeared, Jo and Peter found each other, then asked Jim and Frannie if they wanted to join them for lunch.

# Chapter Thirteen

"I can't believe I ate lunch with Peter. But I wonder if he just asked me because of the fight he had with Sandi," Joleen speculated afterward.

"Not necessarily," said Frannie. "He looked like he was having a great time. And he thought you looked fantastic—like a model."

"Really?" Her eyes widened in disbelief.

Frannie related every comment Peter had made to her. "Didn't you see how he looked at you?" she asked Joleen.

"I can't believe it. I just can't believe it."

That was all Frannie heard from Jo for the next few days as the two girls picked over each day's events with a fine-toothed comb, sharing every detail. Peter sat with Joleen at the beach often, but he still spoke to Sandi sometimes. Frannie was amazed that he hadn't asked Jo out yet, for he seemed so outgoing and popular with his friends. Perhaps he was essentially a slow mover—like Ronnie, she reasoned.

Frannie wrote to Ronnie, telling him about the test commercial and Joleen's successes but not mentioning much about herself— certainly not that Jim had asked her to the Friday night dance. She did, however, add an "I miss you" at the end of the letter and wondered why she hadn't done so before. Was it possible that, in her own way, she held back as much as Ronnie? Or was she just stubborn?

Joleen turned down an invitation to the dance from Jerry Ghio in the hope that Peter might ask her. But he didn't.

"I just want to die!" she lamented. "Why doesn't he ask me out? He doesn't like me, that's why. He's still crazy about Sandi!"

"That's not true!" Frannie insisted. "Go to the dance. It could be that Peter's just trying to wrap up the old relationship gracefully. That can be kind of hard."

"Oh, really? Is that what you're trying to do, too, Frannie?" Joleen quizzed her as she twirled Frannie's honey-blond hair into a sophisticated knot.

Frannie's mouth dropped open in protest at Jo's inference, but she promptly closed it. Was she doing that? Trying to wrap up Ronnie neatly so that she didn't have to deal with him anymore? No, that wasn't it at all. *Ronnie means everything to me—or he used to.* Fear coiled in Frannie's stomach at the very thought. *I've got to see him,* she thought, *see him and talk to him and straighten things out.*

"I don't think you can compare Ronnie and me to Sandi and Peter," she answered stiffly.

"Well, I don't know about that," Jo stated. "The way you and Jim have been lately, it makes me wonder how much you still care about Ronnie. I mean, if I had a boyfriend as attentive as Ronnie, somebody really steady like that, someone I could count on, I'd have everything I ever wanted."

"That's how I used to feel, too, Jo," Frannie replied softly. "I love Ronnie, but when I see you and Peter together, I remember how it used to be with us, and it isn't that way anymore. Like with Jim, everything is new and exciting and romantic. But Ronnie and

I, we're so—we're like an old married couple or something." She felt funny using Jim's words. "We know each other so well, you just wouldn't believe—"

"I think that's romantic in itself," Joleen said, and Frannie remembered how she had missed Ronnie's comfortable predictability the other night when she was with Jim.

"When I found out Peter was a stamp collector, too, I was so excited I couldn't see straight," Jo went on. "I mean, here I already liked him, and then I found out we share more in common than I thought. That's more important than anything else."

"Do you really think so?" Frannie asked, still feeling tremblings of doubt.

She and Ronnie had shared an art interest from the very beginning. Ronnie was and always had been very shy on the outside, but in his artwork, Frannie glimpsed another part of him, a bolder, more vivid person than he outwardly showed himself to be. That had always pleased her and made her feel that she knew something about him no one else knew. And you had to know a person pretty well to know something like that. She wondered if she could ever get past all Jim's bravado and wisecracks to know the real, serious

133

person underneath—the way she had gotten to know Ronnie.

As she stepped into Jim's car, that memory of Ronnie followed her. Joleen had gone to the dance with Jane, and suddenly Frannie wished she'd gone with the girls instead of Jim. Going with a boy demanded light conversation and attention that she wasn't in the mood for.

Jim and Frannie danced the first two numbers, and then Jim wanted to go outside. Remembering the last time, Frannie decided that wasn't a good idea and begged off.

"What's with you, Frannie? You want everything your way, huh?" he snapped, sparks igniting in his eyes.

Reeling from his anger, it took her a second to gather her composure. "If you want some air, Jim, go ahead. I think I'll have some punch."

He grabbed her wrist, and she pulled away, shocked that he would try to force her. Ronnie certainly would never do that. Jim's ruggedly handsome face, the face she had so admired, turned suddenly fierce and sullen as he whirled around and melted into the crowd that choked the entrance. In that moment, Frannie understood the strange feelings she had gotten the night Jim and she had been together. The thrill of his touch laced with a fear and uncertainty that she couldn't identify now suddenly became clear to her: Jim was gorgeous and charming and was used to getting his way. When he didn't, he turned brutal and selfish. Frannie had almost been taken in by him. But as she watched him storm out of the dance, leaving her alone, she realized that she didn't want Jim one bit. And she couldn't help but compare Jim's spoiled attitude to Ronnie's caring ways.

A commotion at the punch table caught her attention. Sandi, her face flushed with anger, was shouting at Peter. "You think you're so great! Well, I just happen to think you're a first-class nerd!" And she flung a cupful of punch at him.

Pink fluid trickled down Peter's horror-stricken face and dripped onto his corduroy shirt. Sandi elbowed her way through the gaping audience and was gone. Peter remained speechless while Jo dabbed at him with napkins. One of the other girls ran to soak a dish towel in water to help mop up the mess.

Finally Peter came to life, his surprise

replaced by fury. "That does it!" he cried, determination hardening his face. "Joleen, I'll be right back. There's some unfinished business I have to attend to."

He was gone for fifteen minutes, and Jo agonized through each one. "What do you think's happening?" she kept asking Frannie. "Do you suppose they'll get back together?"

"I think he just wants to straighten things out," Frannie told her, but she didn't really know. She fidgeted alongside Jo until his return. After all, she was partly responsible for Jo's happiness, having brought all this about. You don't just execute a Popularity Plan for someone and then let them loose with the results—which, Frannie was beginning to see, could often include some disasters.

A few minutes later Sandi swept in on Graham's arm, soon followed by Peter, whose fierce expression changed to a broad smile when he set eyes on Joleen.

Ceremoniously, Peter slipped his arm through Jo's and leaned over to whisper something in her ear. Then he led her out to the dance floor.

Frannie felt herself relax as she looked around at all the contented couples. A terrible longing swept through her as she thought of Ronnie.

"Would you like to dance?"

A tall, dark-haired boy who looked an awful lot like Ronnie waited expectantly for her reply.

"Why, yes. I'd love to."

# Chapter Fourteen

The test commercial Sam Bronson had shot for Kay Nugent jeans had won him the account. "They liked Joleen so much that they're considering using her for the real commercial," Mr. Bronson told Frannie over the phone.

"That's great," said Frannie excitedly. "I can hardly wait to tell her. I wish we could see it."

"I'll tell you what," her father said. "Mort has a Betamax, right? I'll send you a tape. I'm sure Joleen would like to see it."

"Fabulous."

The day that the tape arrived, Joleen, who had been dating Peter regularly since the dance, called him up and invited him to come over to see the tape that evening.

Mrs. Windham had made both a raspberry torte and a chocolate mousse for the occasion. The Windhams, Peter, and Frannie gathered around the TV, talking and laughing excitedly as Mr. Windham pushed the tape into the Betamax.

"Ssshhh! Now here she is! Silence!" Uncle Mort hissed at the rest of the family and Peter, who hunched slightly forward to focus on the flickering TV screen.

Joleen astride the mare was even more compelling on screen than she had been during the shooting. With a toss of her dark hair, she dismounted and stood gazing into Peter's eyes.

"Kay Nugent jeans—the jeans that will fit you like a glove." The announcer's voice dropped a sexy octave lower, and the girls burst out laughing.

They insisted on seeing it again—and again.

"They do make the jeans sound enticing, don't they?" Aunt Joyce twittered, after the sixth showing. She was thoroughly pleased with her daughter's performance. "And to think my shy, lovely daughter did this commercial!"

"I told Uncle Sam I'm next!" piped Jane.

"I want to be a model when I grow up—tall and willowy and graceful." She pranced around the room, fully caught up by her imagination.

Frannie laughed. "Then no more chocolate mousse and raspberry torte!"

From the look of adoration on Joleen's face, Frannie could correctly guess that her cousin would have liked to kiss Peter at that moment—and would have, if her family hadn't been sitting there. Instead, she took a dainty forkful of her mother's celebrational raspberry torte. A dreamy smile played at the corners of her mouth.

"I still can't believe it!" she murmured. "I don't even look like myself!"

"Come on, Jo, stop fishing for compliments—you do, too, and you know it," Jane challenged her, her lower lip stuck out in a cute pout.

Peter and Joleen seemed to be getting along just fine. Sandi and Peter had not spoken to each other again after their argument at the dance.

"She wanted Peter all to herself, which I can't blame her for," Joleen explained afterward. "But she was one of the biggest flirts in town, so why did she have to act so creepy toward him?"

"I guess everyone shows their true colors sooner or later," Frannie mumbled, but she wasn't thinking of Sandi. She was thinking about Jim and how attracted she had been to him until he showed *his* true colors. It was a good lesson for her to learn about other boys—and one that made her appreciate Ronnie even more.

She had been spending her time hiking around the lake with a sketch pad, picking out things like wildflowers and rock formations to draw. Working at the art store, she was able to supply herself with a lot of materials she wouldn't otherwise buy, such as a nice new set of pastels and charcoal pencils and the kind of sketch paper she usually passed up because of its expense. Her dad always maintained that you could sketch on the back of an envelope if you were desperate enough, but Frannie didn't like to get that desperate.

By way of advertisement, Mr. Preston hung a few of Frannie's sketches above the drawing-pencil section in the shop.

"It seems I can't get away from advertising, no matter where I go," Frannie joked to her parents one night on the phone, but they were very proud of her accomplishments.

Then Ronnie's letter came. Frannie held her breath as she slit it open with Aunt Joyce's dragon-tailed letter opener.

A snapshot fell out—a picture of Ronnie's sandcastle contest entry.

Dear Frannie,

I thought you'd like to see this. Won second prize! It was a good contest this year, although that probably sounds real conceited since I won a prize. Too bad you weren't there.

Your job sounds like fun. I guess you're collecting a lot of supplies. That's good. I'm going to be leaving next week for S.F. State so I can get settled into the dorm and get used to everything before school starts. Things are pretty dead around here now anyway. You know how it gets when everyone starts leaving for college. You'll really find out next year when all your friends graduate.

Anyway, I guess I won't see you before I leave, so this is goodbye until I come home again. I'll call you next week.

Love,
Ronnie

Frannie's heart sank like a stone dropped into a pond. She lay on Joleen's spare bed and let her tears come, rolling into her hair in twin, determined paths. She wouldn't see Ronnie for a couple more *months*—not in the week or so she had expected. How could she wait so long?

Suddenly she missed him more than anything in the world. After her dad left, Frannie had suffered a small wave of homesickness, but nothing like this giant wave that engulfed her and carried her off on a tide of self-pitying tears until she felt as limp as old lettuce. What could she possibly do?

When the phone rang, her heart jumped. It was for Joleen. That girl was going to go far. Frannie smiled to herself. *But what about me, and Ronnie?*

Closing her eyes, she conjured up an image of the two of them, their hands slipping out of each other's, and in that floating dream walk, drifting away from one another until each was but a speck on the horizon. She recalled how his hair stuck straight up in the air when it was windy, the way he smiled, sort of crookedly, when he was embarrassed, and how he kissed her—slowly, as if every second counted.

Why had she ever taken his love for granted? For it was she, not Ronnie, who had done so, wasn't it?

Frannie waited until Jo was off the phone, then went to phone him, but hesitated. She couldn't ask him to wait until she got home, for she hadn't been willing to change her plans to suit him. Maybe she could change her plans now and come home early. . . .

She decided to simply call and say hi.

"So how've you been?" he asked. "Did you get my letter?"

Frannie giggled nervously. "Yes, today. I'm surprised that you're leaving early." She worked hard to keep the disappointment out of her voice, but it cracked mid-sentence.

"Yeah, I'm pretty excited about going. I want to check out the place, you know how it is. No sense waiting until the last minute, or it'll be mass confusion up there with all the freshmen trying to find their way around."

"I suppose so." Frannie rattled on about Jo's performance, anxious to fill up what she sensed was a void between them. "And I loved your sandcastle. You deserved first prize," she said, knowing she was overdoing it. He would be blushing right now.

"Yeah, well, I should've sent you a picture of number one. It deserved first." He cleared his throat, saying stiffly, "I'd better got off the line. I'll see you when you get home, sometime."

"OK. And Ronnie—?" Awkwardness loomed between them, not to mention all the disagreements of the past weeks.

"Yeah?"

Frannie ached to say, "I miss you, I really miss you. And I love you, Ronnie." Instead, she said, "Oh, nothing. Take care of yourself." She put the receiver in its cradle.

His plans were already made. She couldn't change them. Had she expected to? And there was no sense in her changing her own plans and going home early. She might really blow it by doing something like that. She'd lost Jim (if she'd ever really had him), and now she was going to lose Ronnie.

"I love you," Frannie whispered to the wall, sobs backing up in her throat.

# Chapter Fifteen

"Why don't you buy Ronnie a present and send it to him when you get home?" suggested Joleen when she heard the devastating news. "Sometimes when words don't make a difference, a gift can."

"You sound like one of those greeting card ads," Frannie said, laughing. "But it's a good idea. I wanted to pick out some art supplies for him. I'll just make a present out of them."

During the week, Frannie studied the store for just the right items. Finally she chose the pastels she'd bought for herself, some canvas, charcoal pencils, acrylic paints, three different kinds of paper, and poster board. It might not seem like a romantic gift to most people, but it was the perfect gift for Ronnie. It would mean more to him than anything else she could buy.

Her parents were arriving in four days to bring her home, but now she wasn't looking forward to going home as much, knowing Ronnie wouldn't be there. In fact, Ronnie must be awfully busy getting settled in, for she hadn't heard a word from him since she'd called, and he had promised to call her.

"There's a vast difference between college and high school," her aunt remarked one day.

Silently, Frannie prayed the difference was not so vast. She might have lost Ronnie altogether.

"Frannie, I don't know how I'm going to manage without you." Joleen hugged her cousin tearfully the afternoon Frannie's parents were due to arrive.

"Joleen, you're perfectly capable of taking care of yourself. Better than me, that's for sure." Frannie checked her bitterness, managing a small smile.

"Come on, Fran. Maybe you can drive up to the city to see Ronnie. There's still time before school starts, isn't there? And anyway," she continued encouragingly, "there're always the weekends. He'll come down to be with you."

"That's if he still cares about me at all," she added, her heart aching for him. Anxious to change the subject, she said, "It'll be nice to see Mom and Dad again. Maybe Dad has another commerical for you." They had learned that Joleen had not gotten the national commercial but she hadn't been upset at all.

"Ha-ha. That was a once-in-a-lifetime thing, I think." Jo laughed.

*That's what my love for Ronnie is—a once-in-a-lifetime thing,* reflected Frannie. *I'll never feel the same about anyone again. It will stand out in my memory as if someone took a snapshot of it. I'll just never lose the feeling.*

"You're leaving me with a different sister," griped Jane. "Next time, you can work on me. I'll be older, and probably fat and ugly."

Frannie gave her a big hug. "You'll never be fat and ugly, Jane. You're fantastic just as you are."

The doorbell rang. The three girls looked at each other. Jane and Jo giggled secretively. Frannie shrugged and slid off the bed to answer it.

When she swung open the door, she gasped.

Ronnie stood on the threshold, his arm leaning against the doorjamb, a huge grin on his face. "Well, aren't you going to invite me in? It's rude to leave a guy standing on the doorstep," he said, teasing.

"Uh, oh, sure," she mumbled. "Wh-what are you doing here? I thought . . ." Frannie searched his familiar features for an answer, although one was slowly sliding into place in her own mind. He looked taller, his shoulders broader, and his face had matured over the summer. His hair curled over the back of his collar now, and a deep tan set off his gray eyes, which met Frannie's astonished gaze with amusement.

"I asked your parents if it'd be OK if I drove to meet you in their place. I decided to wait until next week to go to San Francisco, because—I wanted to see you," he said softly, shoving his hands into his jeans pockets.

She smiled, suddenly transfused with warmth.

"You look different," he said, admiring her in her light-pink slacks and flowered shirt.

"I was just thinking the same thing about you," she replied, laughing. A muffled giggle behind her reminded Frannie of her cousins.

"Hey, there are some people I want you to meet," she said, leading him into the family room, where her cousins and aunt and uncle were posing for the Cheshire Cat Family prize.

Frannie introduced everyone, and after Ronnie was finished shaking hands with them all, Frannie asked, "Did you by any chance have anything to do with all of this?"

Her uncle's laughter bounced off the walls. "Just a teeny bit. We knew he was coming, and it sure was hard to keep a straight face with you moping around here for the last few days, I'll tell you." He and his wife exchanged knowing looks.

Frannie blushed.

"We've heard so much about you," Jane said.

"Frannie told us about your artwork," Joleen put in.

"And you're the one who's so shy?" Ronnie asked her, which was the perfect thing to trigger Joleen's blush glands.

"Not anymore. Not since Frannie came here." She smiled gratefully at her cousin.

Ronnie surreptitiously reached for Frannie's hand and squeezed it. "Yes, I know. Doesn't she have amazing talents?"

The others laughed. Frannie smiled weakly. Her fingers felt like hot wax, and pretty soon she was liable to melt all over the place. Ronnie turned to look at her, and her love for him surged to a pinnacle, rushing in her ears like the sound of the sea. She almost felt like crying.

The Windhams invited Ronnie to stay overnight, since it was such a long trip to make in one day. But Ronnie said he was anxious to get back to take care of some last-minute things before leaving for school. So Frannie's suitcases were stowed in the trunk, farewells were said, and Frannie and Ronnie were on their way. Frannie waved until they turned the corner and the four figures of her aunt, uncle, and cousins dropped from view.

After they'd driven a couple of miles, Ronnie pulled the car over to the side of the road and shut off the engine. He drew Frannie close to him, his voice husky and sweet against her ear.

"I've been wanting to do this for a long time. I guess I never told you how I feel about you enough, Fran. I'm sorry. I guess I figured you just knew."

Lovingly, she traced the curve of his cheek with the back of her hand. "I didn't know,

Ronnie, and I thought the romance was gone. But now I know that we were just changing, that's all. I mean—"

His kisses interrupted her, his mouth pressed firmly on hers while waves of pure ecstasy coursed through her.

Nothing mattered anymore. The summer slipped easily from Frannie's thoughts, to be later encapsulated in memory as the summer she learned what true romance was, that it had seasons of its own that no one could predict.

"I love you, Frannie," Ronnie murmured into her hair.

Funny that Frannie knew it somehow, even before he said so. Yet those very words were so wonderful to hear.

"I love you, too, Ronnie," she whispered, cuddling close, content in the familiar, intoxicating joy of simply being with him.

of lies and confusion—until the night when her lies go too far.

### #17  ASK ANNIE by Suzanne Rand
(#22518-9 • $1.95)

At first, Annie was thrilled to give Tim advice about his girlfriend—until he asks Annie how to keep beautiful, stuck-up Marcy in line. If she helps Tim keep Marcy, Annie will never get a chance with him. But if she doesn't, will Tim stop being her friend?

### #18  TEN-BOY SUMMER by Janet Quin-Harkin
(#22519-7 • $1.95)

Jill's vacation gets off to a wild start when her best friend, Toni, thinks up a contest—who can be the first to date ten new boys! It seems like a great idea until Jill meets Craig and knows she's in love. If Jill drops out of the contest, she won't be able to face her best friend. If she doesn't, she'll lose Craig forever.

### And make sure to look for these
### Sweet Dreams romances, coming soon:

*Read all of these Sweet Dreams romances, on sale now wherever Bantam paperbacks are sold or order directly from Bantam Books by including $1.00 to cover postage and handling and sending a check to Bantam Books, Dept. 503, 414 East Golf Road, Des Plaines, Ill. 60016. Allow 4-6 weeks for delivery. This offer expires 1/83.*

# CIRCLE OF LOVE

O

With Circle of Love Romances, you treat yourself to a romantic holiday—anytime, anywhere. Enter The Circle of Love—and travel to faraway places with romantic heroes....

| | | |
|---|---|---|
| 21502 | GOLD IN HER HAIR | $1.75 |
| 21507 | ROYAL WEDDING | $1.75 |
| 21500 | DESIGN FOR ENCHANTMENT | $1.75 |
| 21510 | THE HEATHER IS WINDBLOWN | $1.75 |
| 21508 | GATES OF THE SUN | $1.75 |
| 21509 | A RING AT THE READY | $1.75 |
| 21506 | ASHTON'S FOLLY | $1.75 |
| 21504 | THE RELUCTANT DAWN | $1.75 |
| 21503 | THE CINDERELLA SEASON | $1.75 |